**Normally Rog...
Rugged Blondness...
Made Him Look Right at Home
in Lake Placid.**

But now he was showing his thirty years. His shoulders were so determinedly square that he reminded Thatcher of a man ready to face the firing squad.

"Maybe you'll think I should have contacted you sooner," he continued painfully, "but I wanted to establish the size of the loss first."

"Loss?" Thatcher prompted him.

"It began after lunch today. I got a courtesy call from the bank at Saranac Lake, warning me that a counterfeit traveler's check had been deposited in one of their commercial accounts yesterday. It was a foreign currency check, and they thought there might be some fakes circulating in Olympic Village. . . . I went through all three vaults, and I fed the number of every single traveler's check into the Telex." He paused to lick his lips, and then his final words erupted in one burst. "Mr. Thatcher, we've taken in a half-million dollars' worth of fakes over our counters."

Books by Emma Lathen

Published by POCKET BOOKS

Most Pocket Books are available at special quantity discounts for bulk purchases for sales promotions, premiums or fund raising. Special books or book excerpts can also be created to fit specific needs.

For details write or telephone the office of the Vice President of Special Markets, Pocket Books, 1230 Avenue of the Americas, New York, New York 10020. (212) 245-6400, ext. 1760.

GOING FOR THE GOLD

EMMA LATHEN

PUBLISHED BY POCKET BOOKS NEW YORK

POCKET BOOKS, a Simon & Schuster division of
GULF & WESTERN CORPORATION
1230 Avenue of the Americas, New York, N.Y. 10020

ISBN: 0-671-43819-0

First Pocket Books printing August, 1982

10 9 8 7 6 5 4 3 2 1

POCKET and colophon are trademarks of Simon & Schuster.

Printed in the U.S.A.

FOR BOB PRIESTLEY,
WHO SO GENEROUSLY OPENED THE RIGHT DOORS
IN MONTREAL AND LAKE PLACID

CONTENTS

GOING FOR THE GOLD

1 BAROMETER FALLING

TIME is money almost everywhere. On Wall Street, the reverse holds true as well. Money shapes the local calendar with ninety-day yields, quarterly dividends and annual reports. Day is done in the financial world when the market closes, not when the sun sets. For most practical purposes, the Copernican system is irrelevant.

But not even Wall Street can dismiss all natural forces. Ultimately sub-zero temperatures, spring floods and summer droughts are reflected in balance sheets and trade deficits, CPI's and COLA's. Accordingly men gather at regular intervals high above the streets of Manhattan to contemplate rainfall in the Ukraine, frosts in Brazil, and the price of fertilizer.

At the Sloan Guaranty Trust they did so twice a year. And despite the importance of these subjects to the third largest bank in the world, the audience of senior Sloan executives was invariably restive.

"I think it's about time to begin. We've dug up some stuff about Common Market pork imports that you'll find interesting," said Walter Bowman, who was chief of research and an incorrigible optimist.

He was happily ensconced behind a mountain of data with two agricultural economists flanking him. At the ready was a large screen upon which charts, tables, graphs and other visual aids were destined to flash.

Resignation blanketed the conference room as inexorably as the snow was falling outside.

"Just a minute, Walter," objected Charlie Trinkam. "Aren't we waiting for John?"

John Putnam Thatcher was senior vice-president of the Sloan Guaranty Trust and the man for whom everybody present worked.

"He's out of town for a couple of days, Charlie," said Bowman, riffling his papers. "Now you all remember the French position on trichinosis—"

But Charlie, who automatically became acting head of the Trust Department during Thatcher's absence, would not let him continue. "Out of town?" he said with pained surprise. "When did this come up—and where did he go?"

"Miss Corsa said something about Lake Placid," Bowman said vaguely. "He took Everett with him."

Rarely had life presented Charlie with such an acceptable excuse for ducking corn–hog ratios. "Well, I'm going to see about this," he said, already scraping back his chair.

Ten minutes later he was casually perched on the corner of Miss Corsa's desk. "Lake Placid? I suppose that means Brad Withers twisted their arms."

John Thatcher's Miss Corsa was a pearl among secretaries. When it came to Bradford Withers, president of the Sloan Guaranty Trust, she was forced to be tactful.

12

"Mr. Withers wanted their opinion about the Sloan operations at the Olympics," she replied.

"Oh, sure," said Charlie with a grin.

His skepticism did not derive from the facts as stated. The Sloan Guaranty Trust was official bank to the Winter Olympics now in progress. Three Sloan branches in Lake Placid, New York, were serving athletes and visitors from forty-two countries, as well as the home-grown thousands converging on the tiny Adirondack community.

"But if anybody's claiming that Brad's keeping tabs on what the Sloan's doing up there in the snow . . ." Trinkam let an eloquent, disrespectful gesture round out the sentiment.

Miss Corsa did not approve. "Mr. Withers was very enthusiastic about having the Sloan named official Olympic bank," she said. "After all, he is a member of the Olympic Committee."

Trinkam snorted. "What did John say about having to dogsled up to this winter wonderland?"

Her faint flush told its own story.

Because, as everybody at the Sloan except Miss Corsa freely admitted, President Bradford Withers, man of many enthusiasms, did not number banking among them. Small boats, big game, first-class hotels and five-star restaurants monopolized most of his attention and virtually all of his time. The Sloan rarely benefited from his counsel or his presence. It took the Winter Olympics to keep him in the continental United States in February. This was not an unmixed blessing.

"Say what you will," Trinkam mused aloud, "when Brad's trotting around Tunisia, he's not dragging John away from the office."

Since no one knew better than Miss Corsa that John Thatcher really ran the Sloan, she did not comment.

"And if the three of them are looking at banks," said Charlie, deeming it time to return to Walter Bowman's recitation, "I'll eat my hat!"

His homburg was safe. Three hundred miles away, John Thatcher was watching the French team practice the soaring perfection of the ninety-meter ski jump. It was a scene of unforgettable brilliance. The sky, ominously grey back at Exchange Place, was a clear blue canopy over the white mountains. Against the cold glitter, multicolored flags snapped in the wind, and gaily clad spectators were silhouetted against the snow.

Color, light and breathtaking performances were all exhilarating.

"Makes you proud to be an American, doesn't it, John?" Brad Withers said happily.

"Yes, indeed," said Thatcher, trying to decipher exactly what Withers had in mind. Since they had just spent an hour watching the West Germans practice, and were now watching the French, it was not simple nationalism. Thatcher decided that it had to be the phenomenon itself. "Lake Placid and the whole committee have done a remarkable job organizing this Olympics," he added, tactfully ignoring last week's mismanaged transportation, ticket sales and award ceremonies.

Withers swelled with pride. "It took a lot of hard work, John. Plus real devotion to Olympic ideals."

"I believe you," said Thatcher, with truth. Prodigies of effort had gone into preparing Lake Placid for this climactic twelve days. Buildings and roads had been built and rebuilt, traffic controls and security systems had been planned and implemented. Everybody from the Federal Government to the Lake Placid High School had labored mightily, so that figure skaters could twirl around the Arena and bobsledders could flash down Mount Van Hoevenberg, while fifty thousand spectators on the spot and untold millions around the world looked on.

Thatcher did not doubt the hard work. Brad's contribution was another matter.

". . . setting a new world record," Withers was saying, as he narrowed his eyes to follow another member of the French team.

"You mean the speed skaters?" asked Thatcher. He and Everett Gabler had been in Lake Placid for barely twenty-four hours, and already they had witnessed six world records being shattered. Maintaining keen interest in tiny increments of distance or speed was increasingly difficult.

"No, no," Withers harrumphed. "The jumps tomorrow morning! It's between the Germans and the French, they tell me. That's why I want to stay to see this new Frenchman—Bisson. He's got a good chance to break the record and beat that German chap—what was his name?"

Thatcher had never heard the blond Viking's name, but he was not called upon to say so.

"Of the German jumpers, no doubt there is that Gunther Euler is *prima.*"

The voice, which came from behind Thatcher, belonged to a sausage-shaped man almost hidden by giant binoculars. The sentence structure misled Brad Withers.

"A very fine young athlete," he said gravely.

This, it developed, was diplomacy misplaced. Mr. Zoffski, Everett Gabler explained meticulously, was not German. He was a sports commentator for Bulgarian National Television.

As such, he was a serious student of the Olympics. It was inevitable, Thatcher decided, that Zoffski should have floated into Gabler's maw. One of the guiding maxims of Everett's life was that, if a thing was worth doing, it was worth doing well. He would have preferred to remain at his desk on Exchange Place. But if duty required his attendance at the Winter Games, then they would be subjected to the same searching analysis he customarily extended to U.S. Steel.

"Yves Bisson," Mr. Zoffski was saying portentously, "he is to the Germans the big thread."

Withers, after worrying about the distinction between *thread* and *threat,* continued on a lofty level. "The American jumpers, I regret to say, are weak this year."

Zoffski paused to let the excitement greeting a fine French jump die down. Then, with the authority of a sports pundit, he said, "Yes, they always are. But in the grand slalom, there you have a good chance."

"Ah, the grand slalom!"

Withers, as Thatcher and Gabler knew to their cost, was capable of now examining prospects of every single forthcoming event. By common consent they both withdrew several paces. With the Sloan's president safely engaged by the Bulgarian expert, it might for once be possible to watch part of the extravaganza that was absorbing an entire township. Elsewhere crowds were watching hockey players and ice dancers. In Olympic Village athletes were resting in their dormitories—or, more likely, lining up in the cafeteria, watching movies, dancing off their surplus energy or reading the *Daily Olympian.* Reporters from all over the world, as witness Mr. Zoffski, were buttonholing coaches and judges. TV cameras were explaining "biathlon" and "luge" to viewers who had never heard of them before. At long last buses were steadily shuttling mufflered crowds from Keene and Saranac Lake. It was a beehive of frenetic activity, purposeful and non-stop.

Thatcher himself had always found banking engrossing. But he had to admit that, when it came to visual effects, Wall Street ran a poor second to the Winter Olympics.

Even practice sessions exerted a special appeal. Here at Intervale, the winter-shortened afternoon was drawing to a close and the sun was beginning to trace long shadows on the snow. It was getting perceptibly colder and Thatcher began shifting from foot to foot. Withers and Zoffski, deep in conversation, were enwreathed by white puffs of frosted breath.

But people were not drifting away, to catch the buses that would transport them back to the fireplaces of their distant lodgings, or to the cheer of their quarters in Lake Placid if they were part of the official Olympic family. Instead, in twos and threes, they were taking up stations from which they could watch the last of the ski jumpers. Huddled in down jackets, turning up their collars, they waited with growing anticipation.

"Ah . . . excuse please . . . it is Yves Bisson just now," said Zoffski, raising his binoculars.

Yves Bisson was a small distant figure at the top of the giant ski tower, crouched over in the taut stillness that touched answering concentration in everyone who watched him.

Then, to the accompaniment of a murmur from the crowd, he was streaking straight down, it seemed, until he spun skyward with impossible smoothness, up and out with a strong, true line.

Despite the ooh's and ah's below, Bisson carried silence with him—up and up. At the height of his arc, he became even more elongated, almost lying on his skis as he stretched for every possible centimeter of glide.

He seemed to hang for a moment, defying gravity with the perfection of his technique. Then suddenly it all went wrong. Bisson crumpled into shapelessness as a great cry went up. He was no longer an arrow, but a helpless ball turning and tumbling, his skis flailing like a windmill.

When he hit the ground, the discipline of athletic competition held firm. The crowd was silent, hoping and praying, while the official first-aid men ran forward. Yves Bisson had landed well short of the run-out area, in deep cushioning snow. Every onlooker was straining to see and to hear, unconsciously waiting for a groan, a twitch. Even a tight contortion of agony would have been welcome.

But the first-aid men knew better. After one look at Yves Bisson, they leaped to their feet and began waving wildly at the crowd.

"He's been shot to death!" one of them screamed. "Run for cover!"

2 HEAVY ACCUMULATION

PANDEMONIUM followed this stark announcement. John Thatcher and Everett Gabler found themselves swept behind a bus as spectators stampeded for shelter. Everywhere they were crouching behind cars and tumbling into service trucks, anything to remove themselves from that austere white background which turned every colored jacket into a perfect target.

"My God!" Thatcher heard one ashen-faced man exclaim. "It's Munich all over again."

Meanwhile the officials, hampered by turmoil and confusion, continued to operate. Thatcher could see them struggling against the tide. The ambulance that had been summoned at the first break in Bisson's performance inched its way through the throng; the attendants jumped down with a stretcher and ran forward. Then they stopped short, the first-aid men gesticulated, and the pool of blood staining the snow grew and grew. A man with a walkie-talkie dashed past, tears streaming down his face, as he pleaded with those in the jumping tower to stay where they were.

Then, incredibly, several competitors wearing skis began to charge off in the direction the first-aid man had indicated. Three security men floundered helplessly in their wake, ordering them not to expose themselves. But suddenly those below realized the meaning of the semaphoring arms barely visible at the top of the tower.

"They can see the sniper!"

Thatcher never knew where the cry came from but its effect was electric. On all sides French and German jumpers went into action following those distant signals. Within minutes a posse was streaming over the hillside. At the same time three carloads of police streaked into the parking lot.

After that it was a matter of organization. Brad Withers was at his very best as he supervised the evacuation of spectators.

"I don't care what the police want," he thundered with remarkable authority. "The important thing is to get these people away from here. John, take those four buses on the right and load them with people going back to Lake Placid. Everett, the ones on the left will go to Saranac."

As the last bus trundled off, the posse began to straggle back to base. Their dejection made it clear that the pursuit had been futile.

"Now before we go," Withers continued, "I want to have a word with these brave boys."

"Brave boys!" snorted the police sergeant in charge. "They could have gotten themselves killed."

"That's why what they did was brave," said Withers firmly.

But the first skiers to arrive disagreed. "We never even saw him," they reported. "He was gone before we started."

Confirmation was forthcoming when the party from the tower was finally allowed to take the elevator down. Their attention had been riveted on Yves Bisson until the walkie-talkie told them there was a killer on the slope. Only then had they scanned the surrounding area. One of them thought he had seen a figure just disappearing into the woodland at the rear. But he could not be sure.

"And there are a bunch of roads and trails back there," said the sergeant in disgust. "So we don't know anything."

"Yes we do," objected a very tall, very fair German who had just skied to a halt. "We found the place where the sniper was. You can see the marks where he was lying."

"Gunther's right," chorused several of the others. "And you can follow his tracks back to the road."

The sergeant was not appreciative. "You could," he said sourly, "before you heroes added another thirty or forty sets."

But the problems of the past were soon displaced by the problems of the future. Before the sergeant could continue, a wiry middle-aged man appeared. At his approach the young skiers all fell back respectfully.

"François Vaux, coach of the French jumping team," he introduced himself. "Do I understand that there is a member of the Olympic Committee here?"

Withers barely had time to agree before Vaux was in full flight. "Our team has suffered a great loss. An hour ago Yves Bisson was alive. Look at him now!"

Involuntarily they all turned to where the body still lay, now surrounded by a corps of police technicians. Brad shook his head sadly. "It's tragic. You have our deepest sympathy at this terrible outrage."

"I don't want condolences. I want protection. What

21

is the Committee doing to prevent this happening again? How many of my team am I going to see this way? Do you think they'll be satisfied with one? Were they satisfied with one at Munich?"

"For God's sake, Vaux!" stammered Withers, appalled at this prospect. "Think what you're saying."

The Frenchman folded his arms. "I am merely being realistic," he growled. "And I repeat, what are you proposing to do about it?"

Thatcher looked on sympathetically. Vaux's concern was more than justified, but it was being aired to the wrong man. Brad could cope with a simple physical threat as he had already proved. But planning ahead, weighing contingencies, minimizing risks were as alien to him in Lake Placid as they were on Wall Street.

"Mr. Withers shares your anxiety," Thatcher intervened. "That is why he wishes to meet with the full IOC so that they can formulate their program as rapidly as possible."

Everett instantly came to his assistance. "And you should be getting your men off this exposed hillside. Isn't there some security at Olympic Village?"

"Of course there is," Vaux snapped.

"Then that's where they should be."

Brad had now recovered his breath sufficiently to close the interview with dignity. "Mr. Vaux, you—and all the other teams—will be hearing from the Committee the minute they've decided what measures to take. In the meantime it makes sense to avoid unnecessary risks."

The French coach was torn. On the one hand, he still wanted to discharge his shocked outrage. On the other hand, he was concerned about the vulnerability of the remaining French jumpers.

"Very well," he finally decided, preparing to leave. "But I shall expect effective action to be taken."

François Vaux was not the only one with unreasonable expectations. By the time the International Olympic Committee met in emergency session later that night, the world-wide media had done their work. Even John Thatcher, pressed into service as Withers' aide, was appalled at the number of institutions stirred to life by the tragic news. Thirty-six embassies had already made representations to the State Department concerning the safety of their nationals. The official security force of the Olympic Games had been displaced, first by the County Sheriff, then by the State Police. Sharpshooters from the FBI were heading north.

Now, if ever, was the time for brilliant executive leadership at the IOC. Unfortunately its president had taken an incautious step on the ice two days earlier, and he was now in an Albany hospital with a broken leg. Officiating in his place was Anthony Melville of Canada. Melville was the IOC's most intransigent foe of the Winter Olympics. According to him, they did not conform to the ancient Greek pattern, they detracted from the Summer Games, and they were a hotbed of commercialism.

"And furthermore they are not representative. Half our members never participate. That's why we're in this mess. Some crazy radicals are protesting a so-called international event that excludes the Third World. And you,"—he paused to glare at the State Police officer who had just delivered his report—"you tell us there's nothing you can do to stop them."

"Not the way you want it," Captain Ormsby said stolidly. "I can protect the competitors all right, but only if they stay in Olympic Village."

"How the hell do you expect us to operate the

Games with all the athletes locked up?" demanded a long-time supporter of the winter event. "Why don't you use some manpower? In Germany they called out the army."

The underlying quarrel had been apparent to John Thatcher for some time. Although the IOC members were addressing their remarks to the police captain, they were actually arguing with each other. Anthony Melville was demanding absolute security for eighteen hundred participants scattered over the countryside. At least half the table was afraid that, when this impossible guarantee was not forthcoming, he would try to call off the Games.

"In Munich you had a hostage situation," Ormsby explained patiently. "There were men with guns in one place that you could attack. We've got one individual who took one shot and beat it. By now he's probably in Canada."

Melville bristled. "Why bring Canada into this?"

"It's the nearest border. He could be there in an hour and a half."

"Canada does not harbor terrorists!"

Thatcher was forced to admire the way Ormsby refused to lock horns with Melville. Instead he used the digression for his own purposes. "I don't think this guy was a terrorist. I think he was hoping we'd all be brainwashed by Munich. But a lot of things point the other way. First off, the ski tracks show there was only one man in there. That's not the way terrorists work."

Brad Withers always had difficulty adjusting to new ideas. "But you said yourself the tracks went back to the road. There could have been accomplices in the car."

"I'm not denying there could have been a wheel man. But terrorists send in an attack team. It makes psychological sense. They keep each other keyed up. Lying belly down in the snow can be a lonely business. Besides, radicals wouldn't have taken one shot. They would have sprayed the place with automatic weapons."

This horrifying possibility silenced everyone at the table except the IOC's public relations man. He was contemplating something worse.

"Do you know what you're saying?" he cried. "The alternative to terrorists is a mad sniper. Can you imagine the effect that will have on spectators? To tell them that somewhere in the snow there's a marksman drawing a bead at random. No sir! I'd rather stick with the Red Brigade."

Ormsby shook his head. "That's not what I'm saying at all. Even though the ground out there was trampled, the security men were still able to get some information. They could see where the sniper's skis were resting, they found some cigarette butts and the marks of the tripod. They figure he was there for over an hour. That means he waited while the German team finished its practice, and he let two French jumpers go by. I think he was out to get Yves Bisson and nobody else."

Brad Withers was indignant. "You're saying the killer followed Bisson over here? Good God, if someone wanted to shoot him in midair, it was just as easy to do it in Europe. They didn't have to cross the Atlantic to ruin our Olympics. I never heard of such a thing in all my life."

While Brad gobbled, Thatcher was considering this new approach. "I doubt if it was sheer perversity on the sniper's part. If you look at it from his point of view, there were distinct advantages. Killing Bisson in France would have brought the local police down on his relatives and acquaintances. But here? Even if the authorities are ninety percent convinced that the motive is personal, they still have to take precautions against a political plot. Inevitably a good deal of their attention will be diverted toward protecting the remaining competitors, reviewing the movements of known terrorists, cooperating with the State Department. Why, even dealing with their own communications . . ." Thatcher let his voice trail away as he bobbed his head apologetically.

Ormsby did not take offense. "You're right, Mr. Thatcher. We've already got ten men doing liaison work full-time. But sooner or later we'll get information from Paris. Sooner or later we'll get flight lists. Already we've come up with something interesting over at—"

He was interrupted by a harried secretary. "Mr. Roger Hathaway," she said, "insisted that he see Mr. Withers and Mr. Thatcher at once."

"Ah," murmured Brad, gratified. "Roger has heard about our trouble and he's offering to help."

"I doubt if he's come about Bisson," said Thatcher. The Sloan's manager in Lake Placid had other fish to fry. "There must be trouble at the branches."

Their visitor was right on the heels of the secretary. "I'm afraid it's both," he announced from the doorway.

Normally Roger Hathaway's rugged blondness and lean vigor made him look right at home in Lake Placid. But now he was showing his thirty years. The tight frown creasing his forehead was echoed by a score of tiny wrinkles at his temples, and his eyes were red with fatigue. His shoulders were so determinedly square that he reminded Thatcher of a man ready to face the firing squad.

"Maybe you'll think I should have contacted you sooner," he continued painfully, "but I wanted to establish the size of the loss first."

He had sounded a tocsin.

"Loss?" Thatcher prompted him.

"It began after lunch today. I got a courtesy call from the bank at Saranac Lake, warning me that a counterfeit traveler's check had been deposited in one of their commercial accounts yesterday. It was a foreign currency check, and they thought there might be some fakes circulating in Olympic Village. So I got busy on a memo to the home office asking them to verify our receipts. But then the second call came through, and I decided to start with what we have here. That's what I've been doing ever since. I went through all three vaults, and I fed the number of every single traveler's check into the Telex." He paused to lick his lips, and then his final words erupted in one burst. "Mr. Thatcher, we've taken in a half-million dollars' worth of fakes over our counters."

Thatcher did not make an immediate reply; he was too busy running down an appalling list of possibilities.

Withers was not operating under the same burden. But the Sloan presence in Lake Placid had been his own particular brainchild and any threat to its success moved him.

"I thought you said this had something to do with the murder," he complained.

"I'm coming to that." Hathaway cast an uneasy glance at Thatcher's frozen countenance before plunging ahead. "The second call was from Saranac after they heard about the shooting. They wanted me to know that their fake check was passed in the name of Yves Bisson."

The International Olympic Committee was not slow to realize that Roger Hathaway was dispelling the specter of a terrorist invasion. They were openly relieved to trade in radical assassins for professional criminals.

In the outburst of self-congratulation that followed, John Thatcher found Captain Ormsby at his elbow.

"Now, I call that real interesting," Ormsby began. "Especially when you consider what we found in Bisson's room. You know, Mr. Thatcher, we've sent away to Albany for a financial expert, but I'll bet you could tell us as much as any outsider."

Thatcher was very grim. "And if it has anything to do with traveler's checks, I have a half-million-dollar inducement to cooperate."

"Well, why don't you come and see for yourself."

3 DEGREE DAYS

AN hour later Thatcher was ready to start work. Almost half that period had been spent gaining admission to Olympic Village. The security precautions now reigning made a mockery of Everett Gabler's earlier question to the French jumping coach. After they had driven seven miles west from Lake Placid on the road to Saranac, Thatcher had expected something resembling a gigantic country club. Instead he found a barren rural site in the center of which lay a newly constructed compound of nine buildings. The entire complex was surrounded by a double-fence system enclosing a broad swath of ground. Armed units were patrolling the flood-lit outer perimeter. Guard dogs were running between the fences. Jeeps bristling with paramilitary personnel swept along surrounding trails.

"Good God!" exclaimed Thatcher. "It looks like a prison."

Ormsby was amused. "It is. Didn't you know? That's how the town got this place free. They agreed to have a new federal prison here if they could use it first for the Olympics. I hear that a lot of participating countries didn't like the idea." Then he sobered. "But it's been a godsend today. All we had to do was implement the federal plans."

Thatcher was sorry that Everett had missed this experience. Gabler would have been genuinely interested in a new approach to financing temporary housing. But Everett was busy extracting the sad details from Roger Hathaway.

Their first stop had been the security building at the gates. Tonight there was no nonsense about flourishing ID's. Phone calls had been made to the State Police and to the IOC. Then, past the gates and the dogs, was the administration building and a further check. Ormsby made no attempt to hurry the process.

"When you set up a procedure, you want to encourage them to follow it," he explained as they waited to be escorted across the compound. "I'm surprised you haven't been here before. Your bank is over there with the Post Office and the Medical Center."

Obediently Thatcher looked toward the darkened expanse. His interest in short-lived branches was minimal. Long-term losses were something else again.

Ormsby continued his role as guide when they were finally ushered along the brilliantly lit path toward the dormitory buildings in the rear.

"That's their entertainment center. It's got a disco," he said unnecessarily, indicating windows from which pulsating sounds and lights were flowing. "And movies and game rooms and God knows what else."

A particularly vibrant chord sounded, accompanied by enthusiastic yells and stampings.

"I'm glad to see that the young people aren't letting the situation depress them," Thatcher remarked.

Ormsby was a veteran of many disasters. "It's always

that way. You'd be surprised how fast most people get back to business as usual."

Further proof of this truth was waiting at Dormitory H. Here the usual reception committee of security guards had been reinforced by a band of athletes ready to sound the alarm and to stage a delaying action. But beyond the entrance everything seemed normal. As they passed the doorway of a lounge, they could see a group clustered around the bright screen of a television set from which no sound came.

"I wonder what they're watching with the audio off," Thatcher murmured.

"Themselves," Ormsby replied as they mounted the stairs to the second floor. "All the dormitories have a television playback system. That way they can analyze their own performance and get tips from their teammates. Well, here we are. This is where Bisson was staying."

He barely gave Thatcher an opportunity to glance at the twin-bedded cubicle. Upon signal, the trooper on duty produced a stack of traveler's checks and a magnifying glass.

"This is what I wanted you to look at," Ormsby invited.

It did not take Thatcher long to arrive at his conclusion. "There really isn't any doubt. This one folder is genuine and the rest are counterfeit. The rag content is quite different."

"That's what we thought," Ormsby nodded. "We didn't know about the rag content, but we noticed that most of them didn't have any signature at all while that particular flap had been signed in one corner. I assume these foreign traveler's checks work like American Express?"

"Almost exactly. On a bona fide sale of Eurochecks,

the customer signs when he makes the purchase and then countersigns whenever he cashes one. I see that Bisson has Eurochecks in three currencies here—French francs, German marks and Swiss francs. Hathaway will be able to tell us if that accords with what we've taken in."

Ormsby did not want Thatcher to think that the State Police were not doing their share. "And we'll get on to the other banks in the area. They may have been hit, too."

"I doubt it." Thatcher had been pondering Roger Hathaway's disclosure. "You may not realize this, Captain, but the Sloan opened here in Lake Placid because the Olympic Games were bringing in a volume of foreign visitors and foreign currencies that the local banks were not equipped to handle. Now, the counterfeiters obviously decided to capitalize on this situation by passing their fakes where they would seem to be normal transactions. They probably had a whole gang of people like Bisson ready to go into action at the same time. And the others did go into action today. The only thing I don't understand is how that stray check turned up a day early in Saranac."

"It may not be the only one. Tell me what you think of this." Ormsby was crossing to the other side of the room. Until now their attention had been centered on the belongings of Yves Bisson. "While we were searching the room we went through the roommate's side, too. Here are his traveler's checks."

Thatcher flipped through the folder, counting. Then he meticulously studied each check. "The first ten are all right. But the last five are not. And although I'm no expert, I'd say the last five signatures are forgeries as well."

Ormsby agreed. "That's how I make it. I think

Bisson couldn't resist the temptation to do a little substituting. Why don't we hear what the roommate has to say?"

But they soon realized that Raoul Thibault was not going to be any help. When he was shown his folder of checks, he beamed. When he was told there were fifteen left, he looked sad. When the discontinuity in numbers was mentioned, he was blank.

"Still," Thatcher persisted, "when you cashed the eleventh check, you would have guessed something was wrong, wouldn't you? Because its number wouldn't match your list."

"My list?" Thibault repeated suspiciously.

"The list of numbers you keep for your own protection."

Thibault, however, had lost patience. "I know nothing of numbers. When I want money, I sign in this corner and they give me money. When I have no more checks to sign, I have no more money. Numbers are not necessary." Conscious of a certain lack of enthusiasm from his audience, he suddenly smiled brilliantly. "It is really very simple."

"You see what I mean, Mr. Thatcher," Ormsby sighed. "If Bisson played his games on others, you could have quite a few innocent passers of fakes. Enough so you ought to be careful whose traveler's checks you take."

Thatcher was at his driest. "I can promise you that any Eurocheck presented to the Sloan will receive very thorough scrutiny, Captain. But none of this explains Bisson's check. Unless you think Bisson himself was not at Saranac."

For the first time Thibault showed glimmers of intelligence. "Yves was near Saranac yesterday, if that is what you mean."

"You're sure?"

"Well, he said so. He and Suzanne Deladier were talking about it at lunch."

This was all that Ormsby needed. "Do you know where I can find her?"

"I just left her. The whole French team is in emergency meeting. In case of more attacks, you understand."

"You mean she's on the team?"

If Ormsby had been scornful of Thibault's financial methods, that scorn was now returned with interest.

"Suzanne Deladier," Thibault repeated, shocked at such ignorance. "The figure skater."

When Suzanne Deladier appeared, it was hard to believe that she was a consummate athlete. Thatcher knew enough about the Olympics to appreciate that any competitor had whipcord muscles, knife-edge reflexes and superhuman stamina. But Suzanne, who admitted to all of nineteen years, was a tiny, fine-boned creature with translucent fair skin, velvety dark eyes and raven hair. She spoke fluent English with a marked British accent. She was not alone.

"Coach Vaux insisted on coming along," she explained demurely. "To protect me."

He was still on his mettle. "I do not understand why the police wish to interrogate Suzanne about a terrorist attack, but I am here to see that she is not imposed upon. Tomorrow there will be somebody from the French Embassy."

"Good. I'm glad the youngsters are being looked after," Ormsby said mildly. "But you can stop worrying about a terrorist campaign. Bisson seems to have been mixed up in some criminal activity. That is the likeliest motive for his murder."

The effect on Vaux was immediate.

"But this is outrageous! You may wish to prevent panic here in Lake Placid, but that is no justification for defaming a dead man. I've known Yves for over two years, and there was no finer sportsman, no more generous competitor."

Ormsby held up a pacifying hand. "Now let's get this straight, Mr. Vaux. Bisson was mixed up in something. Maybe he was a participant, but maybe he was innocently involved," he said, suppressing all reference to Raoul Thibault's checkbook. "There's no way we can tell until we know what went on at Saranac."

"Saranac?" Little Miss Deladier was interested.

Ormsby turned to her quickly. "You and he went there yesterday?"

"We all did."

Before a worried François Vaux could intervene, Ormsby pressed forward. "You mean there was a whole group? You and he were not alone?"

"Of course not." There was the slightest suggestion of disdain in her voice. "It was a celebration really. The boys who came out high in the standings after the first half of the jumping arranged it. None of us had ever ridden snowmobiles before. Yves had heard of this place outside Saranac where you could rent them and ride on miles and miles of track. It was wonderful."

"And how did you pay for the rental?"

Suzanne's eyes widened. "I have no idea. I suppose one of the boys did."

"Perhaps you'd better tell me who else was there."

"Let me think." Suzanne wrinkled her nose thoughtfully. "It was all very informal. We met together at the shuttle bus. I know Gunther Euler helped arrange it. Tilly Lowengard was there. Oh yes, and Dick Noyes was with her."

Thatcher and Ormsby looked at each other. The enlargement of the outing to Saranac cut both ways. In the confusion of five or six people milling about, everybody could claim to have noticed nothing. On the other hand, the potential number of witnesses had increased.

Ormsby pushed himself to his feet. "We'd better start rounding them up. I'm going to want to talk with everybody who went on this trip."

Almost immediately he ran up against the realities of life in Olympic Village. His request for a small group of skiers and skaters produced a buzzing cloud of coaches, trainers and delegation bigwigs. They were bewildered, incredulous, pained, but above all, they were adamant.

"Not on your life," said an American coach roundly. "It was hard enough getting my boys out of the disco and into the sack. I sure as hell won't get any of them up now."

"Perhaps I am misunderstanding you, Captain Ormsby," murmured a tidy German who had shattered five world records in his younger days.

The Swiss was not so polite. "Do you realize that it is after eleven-thirty?" he demanded.

Ormsby tried to justify himself. "Look, I was just talking to Suzanne Deladier, and she wasn't in her nightie. What is all this?"

The French, everybody told him, were the exception. Fearing attack, they had preferred not to scatter their forces.

"But now that there is no longer any question of terrorists," said the Swiss, "they, too, have retired."

Ormsby bowed to the inevitable. But it then developed that the undisturbed slumber of his witnesses was not the only impediment facing him. Tomorrow's agenda was crammed with practice sessions, competition and transport to distant places. Access to any one Olympian was difficult; access to five of them at once seemed impossible.

Making the necessary arrangements, Thatcher foresaw, was going to take time.

"Let me know when you finally corral them all," he said, rising to leave.

Ormsby looked up from his calculations. "I will," he said, "and thanks for your help, Mr. Thatcher. I'll have one of the boys run you back to your motel."

That, however, was not where Thatcher was headed. These police inquiries had been no more than a busman's holiday.

"I want to look in on Gabler and Roger Hathaway," he said, responding to Ormsby's open curiosity. "The Sloan's going to be doing a little digging of its own, Captain."

Twenty minutes later, a cruiser deposited him at the Sloan's local command post, a one-time Victorian summer home, gracing a hillside on the outskirts of town. Turrets, porches and gables abounded and, by moonlight, evoked the statelier past. But appearances were misleading. In recent years every other season had brought a new couple eager to turn this relic into a charming country inn or a cozy ski lodge. Since blueberry pancakes can do only so much, a three-month lease by the Sloan Guaranty Trust was the best thing that had happened to the Andiron Inn since William Howard Taft.

The arrangement was not working out badly for the Sloan, either. As lights blazing at innumerable windows attested, the Inn provided twelve much-needed bedrooms for the Sloan staff. Downstairs there were parlors and dining rooms where Sloan customers could be wined and dined in comfort, if not elegance. Another advantage was the self-contained owner's apartment which provided some semblance of normalcy for Roger Hathaway.

The rental charge for these conveniences had startled even Bradford Withers. At the moment Thatcher was more interested in another large sum of money.

A vaguely familiar young man answered the bell, opening the door onto a large foyer dominated by stained glass and ski racks.

He insisted on guiding Thatcher. "You see, the real entrance to Roger's place is around by the side," he explained, heroically stifling a yawn, "but you can get there from here. Only it isn't easy."

It was, in fact, an obstacle course. Thatcher lost count of the massive fireplaces, unexpected staircases and oversized sofas they passed. Each room had a piano, a stuffed moosehead, or both.

Hathaway's apartment came as a relief. Living room, bedroom, kitchen and bath were simply but brightly furnished. One wall was covered with a magnificent aerial photograph of Lake Placid, and there was a pot-bellied stove in the corner.

Even the clutter of Hathaway's life struck a welcome note: ski boots heaped carelessly near the door, a pile of records—in and out of sleeves—near the hi-fi. The desk at the window held a portable typewriter and a pile of business papers.

Inevitably that was where Everett Gabler had chosen to station himself.

"Ah, John," he said severely.

"Olympic Village took more time than I expected," said Thatcher while Hathaway helped him out of his coat.

38

"Did Ormsby come up with anything?" Hathaway asked.

"We may have explained how and why Bisson's counterfeit Eurocheck came to light in Saranac," said Thatcher, removing his scarf.

The snowmobile saga kept Hathaway motionless with Thatcher's belongings draped over his arm. Everett was less impressed.

"Confirmation, as if we need it, of a considerable counterfeit scheme," he snorted. "Five athletes—"

"No, no, Everett," Thatcher hastened to say. "You're being premature. Of course, something may come to light when Ormsby speaks to them tomorrow, if he ever rounds them all up. But at the moment, the presumption is that they were no more than witnesses. Which reminds me, Hathaway. Did you know Bisson? Or—" he dug out a note he had made for himself—"or the rest of them? Dick Noyes, Tilly Lowengard . . ."

Hathaway was jamming Thatcher's coat into an already overstuffed closet. "No, I haven't met many of the competitors," he said. "They got here late. I did meet some of the Olympic officials who were setting things up."

"Well, then," said Thatcher, handing the scrap to Gabler. "I think this is your baby, Ev. You can add it to your list."

He was perfectly confident that Everett had a list. But mindful of the awkwardness of Hathaway's position, he waited until the younger man rejoined them before continuing. "Now, what have you two been doing?"

For all his quirkiness Gabler, too, comprehended Hathaway's predicament. So, with rare self-effacement, he let a subordinate hold the floor.

"We held a meeting for the whole staff," said Hathaway, explaining the yawn that had greeted Thatcher. "We showed some of the stuff to everybody. You noticed the rag count? Well, from here on in, I think I can safely say nobody's laying off any queer on the Sloan."

"If there's any more out there," Thatcher interjected. "It looks very much like a one-shot operation."

With a dispirited shake of the head, Hathaway accepted this without argument. "But I've got to admit that before this happened, I would have sworn this was impossible."

"Tsk, tsk!" said Everett. "Still, crying over spilled milk won't get us very far."

Thatcher was less Spartan. "Yes, we have to be thinking of the other steps the Sloan should be taking. Ev, I think you'd better get back to New York as soon as possible."

"Exactly what I thought," said Gabler promptly. "I've ordered a car which should be here in another half-hour."

Thatcher, who had been thinking in terms of an early morning flight, tried to measure up. "Excellent. Now, you'll want to get in touch with Eurocheck. Also, we should ask around banks in New York—and Montreal, too, I suppose—to see if they've encountered any problems. And I expect we'd better get some currency experts up here to study what we've got sitting in the vault. Then I'd like you to make some inquiries about those names I gave you."

None of this came as a surprise to Everett.

"One more thing," said Thatcher, glancing toward Hathaway. "Regrettable but necessary, I'm afraid. We'd better double check the personnel file of every single

Sloan employee here in Lake Placid, just in case. See if there are any local connections, Olympic connections —anything."

At this, Roger Hathaway was thunderstruck. "My God!" he said, dismayed. "I never thought of *that!*"

Reverting to form, Everett was astringent. "A credit to your heart—but not to your head."

4 CLOUD COVER

BY dint of great perseverance, Captain Ormsby finally managed to settle on a time the following morning when five Olympic schedules could accommodate a murder investigation. Ten-thirty, he was assured, was the only possible moment.

Strictly speaking, this was not true. While the high-level dickering went on, the young people had put their heads together. As a result, at seven-thirty the next morning, they picked up their breakfast trays and cornered a table in the Olympic cafeteria. The three men, who lived in different dormitories within the compound, had had no opportunity for conversation. Tilly Lowengard, on the other hand, lived on the same floor of the women's quarters as Suzanne Deladier. She was complaining that this advantage had been futile.

"Suzanne says there's nothing to tell," she appealed to the others, "but she must have learned something from the police last night."

The two girls could not have been more different. Tilly had a short crop of brown curls that was almost always tousled from exercise, the outdoors, or her habit of tweaking stray strands in moments of excitement. Practicing for the Swiss women's slalom team had left her with windburned cheeks and a fine collection of bruises. Although she was two years older than Suzanne, she seemed younger when her bursts of impulsive enthusiasm caromed off the French girl's controlled elegance.

"Haven't you heard the rumors, Tilly?" asked the man sitting next to her. "All over the Village they're saying that Yves was up to his neck in something criminal."

Tilly's eyes widened. "Gunther!" she protested. "You don't mean something seriously criminal, do you?"

Gunther Euler shrugged. "If it involved murder, that is certainly serious enough for me."

"You guys have got to be kidding! You're trying to tell me that Yves was into something really crooked? Where in hell would he get the time?"

This involuntary explosion came from Dick Noyes. He was the only American present and the only true amateur. The others were all world-class competition athletes, familiar figures on the international circuit. Dick was the lowliest member of the low-ranked American downhill team. A series of last-minute wins had sent him to Lake Placid, but the serious business of his life was studying to become a veterinarian. Juggling the demands of his training schedule and his college career was a constant strain. For the others, the 1980 Winter Olympics would be a victory only if they brought home a medal or broke a world record. For Dick Noyes, the victory was being there.

"We are not certain of anything as yet. Suzanne, you had better tell us what you know."

The air of quiet authority came naturally to Carlo

Antonelli. At thirty he was not only a good deal older than his companions, he was also an Olympic veteran. This was his third try with the Italian bobsled team.

Suzanne had been quietly eating breakfast while the others spoke. Even this simple act was marked by her ballet training. As she spooned oatmeal, her wrist gracefully led the upward movement. She did not reply directly.

"It is very mortifying, being singled out for police attention," she said.

"Well, you can relax now," Dick Noyes told her bracingly. "Now they're after all of us."

Suzanne was not grateful. "If I had not agreed to go snowmobiling in Saranac, I would not be involved. That is what the police want to ask questions about."

"So that's why they selected us." Carlo Antonelli ignored Suzanne's lament. "I do not understand what crime Yves could have committed on that trip, but since we were with him . . ."

"You may be offended by this development, Suzanne. Personally I am relieved," Gunther Euler confessed. "Naturally I am sorry about Yves. But it is not so pleasant, flinging yourself into the snow and being afraid that someone is about to shoot you."

Antonelli studied him appraisingly. "I had forgotten that you were present when Yves was killed."

"As was the entire German jumping team," Euler reminded him. "And I can tell you, our performance would suffer if every time we jumped we were afraid of becoming targets for a marksman."

This effectively silenced everyone except Tilly Lowengard, who had been following her own train of thought.

"It's just occurred to me, Gunther. Do you realize that you're now in the lead for the combined jumping?"

A spot of color appeared on Euler's cheek, but his voice did not falter.

"Yes. I had thought of that."

Three hours later he was again under fire.

"Mr. Euler, I understand that you and Yves Bisson arranged this trip to Saranac. Is that correct?" Ormsby was asking.

Gunther Euler was untroubled as he faced the police captain and John Thatcher.

"It depends what you mean by arranged. On Monday, Yves and I finished first and second in the standings for the ski jump." He grinned unashamedly as he went on to explain: "That was good because there was only one more round to go. One of us would certainly win the gold on Friday. And because of the gap the coaches were giving us a free day on Tuesday. So, when we were sitting in the disco on Monday night, we decided to celebrate. We'd get a group together and go snowmobiling."

"I understand all that. But why Saranac? There are snowmobiles in Lake Placid."

"There are also sixty thousand people," Euler retorted. "We wanted to get away from it all and find some space."

"All right." Ormsby pressed on. "Let's go back to Monday night. How were you going to get a group together?"

Euler blinked. "By asking people to come with us. Yves said he was going to ask Suzanne. We could see her dancing on the other side of the room."

Suzanne Deladier did not wait for Ormsby to question her. "Yes, it must have been shortly afterwards that Yves invited me."

"He asked me at the disco also," Carlo Antonelli volunteered. "It was late, just before I left."

Wordlessly Ormsby swiveled to the remaining couple.

"Dick and I were having breakfast Tuesday morning when Yves mentioned snowmobiling," Tilly Lowengard remembered. "I've forgotten how it came up."

Dick Noyes frowned in his efforts at recollection. Rugged and chunky, he looked to Thatcher as if he would be a strong skier rather than a graceful one. It was easy enough to imagine Gunther Euler as a bird in flight. Noyes would be more likely to bash through obstacles than to soar over them.

"We were talking about schedules," he finally decided. "The slalom practices were in the morning, and we were wondering what we'd do in the afternoon. That was when Yves leaned across the table and invited us to go along. He said Suzanne and Gunther were coming, too."

Ormsby nodded, then turned to the German. "Mr. Euler, if you were both going to collect people for this expedition, how come everybody here was asked by Bisson?"

"He was luckier than I was," Euler said placidly. "I did talk to two or three persons, but most of the downhill racers and the cross-country men were all tied up."

Ormsby, Thatcher was pleased to see, did not intend to linger over preliminaries. Without pausing he swept forward to his main concern. "Once you got to this place, did you do anything besides snowmobile?"

They all stared at him, then burst out laughing. Dick Noyes was the first to recover. "Sorry, Captain, I guess you haven't seen Twin Forks. It's nothing more than a crossroads outside Saranac. There's a dinky motel and, across the highway, a garage that rents snowmobiles. We rented three snowmobiles, spent a couple of hours on the logging trails, and then caught the shuttle bus back here. What's all the fuss about?"

"There's no fuss. I simply want to get the details straight. Such as how you paid for the rental."

This simple remark produced a volley of replies as everyone burst into speech. Ormsby had touched a sore spot.

"Yves wouldn't let anyone else share the tab." Dick Noyes was still resentful. "I tried, Carlo tried, even Tilly tried. The only one he'd talk to was Gunther."

Euler expanded on this. "It was a challenge, you understand. Yves said the winner of the jumping should pay and, as he was going to win, it would be his party. If I won he would have to accept repayment."

But from all the babble a very clear picture emerged. There had been nothing furtive about Yves Bisson's behavior. He had flourished his Olympic credentials in order to persuade the garage owner to accept a Eurocheck. Everyone had been a witness to his crime.

Or almost everyone. Thatcher narrowed his eyes as he inspected Suzanne Deladier. She was sitting slightly apart, quietly contained and removed from the conversation. According to her testimony the previous evening, she had not even noticed who paid for the rental. There was no question of her having joined in the friendly squabble. Of course, she might simply be an old-fashioned girl, depending on the nearest man to pick up the check. But there was more to it than that. There was a quality that left her untouched by the good-natured, rowdy high spirits around her. With a sudden flash of insight, Thatcher realized that it was a question of brownness. Tilly Lowengard, for instance, was undeniably brown. She had brown curls, sparkling brown eyes and a golden brown skin. The others ran the gamut from Dick Noyes' ruddy weather-beaten com-

plexion to Carlo's swarthiness to Gunther's deep life-
guard tan. They carried with them great gusts of fresh
air. But Suzanne was a Dresden shepherdess. Thatcher
was willing to bet she was a city girl.

Meanwhile Ormsby was bringing the story of Twin
Forks to its conclusion. He now had everybody on the
shuttle bus for the voyage home.

"But what's there to tell?" Dick Noyes complained.
"It was just like any other bus ride. We were all talking
and joking. Nothing happened."

"That's right," Tilly corroborated. "Even when I
thought Yves was sick, it turned out he wasn't. Or at
least he said he wasn't."

"Oh, come on, Tilly," Dick scoffed. "He knew,
didn't he?"

Ormsby was willing to grasp at any straw. "What's
this about Bisson being sick?"

Tilly was only too willing to tell him. "We were all
talking about whether we'd be able to see the downhill
racing. But we all had different practice sessions, and
Yves became impatient at how complicated it was getting. He yanked the printed schedule from his pocket
and began to straighten us out. Then suddenly he bent
forward with a little moan, and all the things he'd
pulled from his pocket began to slide to the floor. I
really thought he was going to be sick right there."

John Thatcher began to see light. He leaned forward.
"Tell me, Miss Lowengard," he asked gently, "were
his traveler's checks among the things he pulled out?"

"Yes. He was stuffing them back while he said he
was all right."

"He probably had a muscle twinge," Noyes insisted.
"After all, he put in a hard day on Monday."

Tilly was exasperated. "For heaven's sake, Dick, if
that had been it, Yves would have been back to normal.

But he was like a ghost from then on. And you remember how lively he was until then, how he was joking with Coach Vaux when we brought the snowmobiles back and how he teased Suzanne—"

Captain Ormsby's head had come up sharply.

"What's that about Coach Vaux?" he demanded, dangerously quiet. "Do you mean he was on this trip to Twin Forks and nobody told me?"

Tilly shook her head. "But he didn't go with us. He was just there. We ran into him when he and that girl were coming out of the coffee shop."

"What girl, Miss Lowengard?" Ormsby asked evenly.

"Her name was Katarina something. She works in administration. Oh, Gunther, she was German. Maybe you remember her name."

"Katarina Maas," he supplied.

Ormsby took a deep breath. "And were they around while you were paying for the rental?"

"Well, they must have been. They were still there when we ran for the bus."

Ormsby's face was etched into lines of anger. "Goddam that man. He was sitting right there last night when I said I wanted to speak to everyone who was at Twin Forks. Well, he's not going to get away with this."

"You said you were interested in the trip, Captain," Vaux said stubbornly. "How was I to know you meant something else?"

"Don't try to split hairs with me, Vaux. You knew I was interested in everyone who saw Bisson at Twin Forks."

"That isn't what you said."

Ormsby glared at him. "Well, now that we've got you admitting you were at Twin Forks, suppose you tell us what you were doing there."

49

"I wasn't doing anything in particular. Tuesday was a free day and I wanted to get away. So I took the bus to see something of the surrounding countryside. Miss Maas happened to be sitting across the aisle from me. When we pulled up at Twin Forks, I noticed the sign for the restaurant in the motel. So I suggested to her that we have a cup of coffee and maybe stretch our legs. That's all."

"Except for the fact that you happened to run into Yves Bisson there."

François Vaux shrugged. "Yes. He and the others had been snowmobiling. I have no idea where they went or how long they'd been gone."

"Never mind that," Ormsby rasped irritably. "The point is that you were there when Bisson paid for the rental."

"I don't remember that."

Ormsby was triumphant. "We've got witnesses. You were there when they returned. You were still there when they caught the bus."

"Possibly. I have no recollection of the transaction. I was busy talking to Suzanne Deladier. She was a little out of things. Then when they left, Miss Maas and I strolled about until the next bus."

"Wonderful," Ormsby snorted. "So your story is that you took a bus ten miles to have a cup of coffee and take a walk through the same snow they've got here."

"It was very beautiful," Vaux said stolidly.

"He's lying," Ormsby announced.

"And he intends to go on doing it," Thatcher agreed.

"The thing that burns me up is that he may have a simple reason. The record shows that he's got a wife and three children back in France. He could have been

50

taking a girl to a motel for the oldest reason in the world."

Thatcher nodded. "But if he isn't going to tell you, it's unlikely that Miss Maas will."

"Oh, he cleared his story with her last night. I could tell that. What's more, he isn't the only one in that bunch who's lying. Anything strike you about their stories?"

It was almost an embarrassment of riches. "Certainly. Miss Deladier, Gunther Euler and Carlo Antonelli."

Captain Ormsby was regarding Thatcher with new approval. "Not much gets by you, does it?" He raised three fingers to recapitulate. "Little Miss Deladier told us last night she was joining a big group. But according to the timetable, none of the others had been invited when she agreed to come. At that time there was only Bisson and Euler. Which means she may have been a lot more intimate with Bisson than she's letting on. After all, they're both from France.

"Then there's Antonelli. He was very quick to tell us that Bisson invited him. Too quick. Because Bisson didn't mention him when he spoke with Noyes and Tilly Lowengard the next morning. If Euler invited him, they have some reason for hiding their association.

"And just on the surface, that makes sense. A lot of these people have never met each other before. It's only in the Olympics that you get all these different events in the same place." Ormsby had done his homework on winter sports. "You can have a World Cup skating match in Vienna, the European ski championship in Switzerland and the International Ski Jump in Norway. But the one person that Bisson had to bump up against all the time was Euler."

"And Vaux," Thatcher reminded him. "Which makes

what I have to tell you very odd, Captain. Has anyone mentioned that Vaux and Euler both turned up yesterday at Intervale after the spectators had been evacuated from the ski jump area? I saw them myself."

"I didn't know that." Ormsby subjected this new information to critical appraisal. "But I don't see what's odd about it. Vaux would naturally be watching his boys practice, and most of the German team hung around after their turn."

"Of course they should have been there," Thatcher agreed. "But why didn't I see them earlier? Vaux in particular. If he'd tackled Brad fifteen minutes sooner, he'd have an alibi. Now Euler told us he was with the posse that chased up the hillside. If that's true, he should be in the clear."

Ormsby whistled softly. "That's a nice point. I'll get some questions started to everybody else who was there. But the really interesting thing is that neither of those beauties said a word about seeing Bisson shot."

Thatcher thought back to the two witnesses, the relaxed German and the determined Frenchman. On the surface, what a contrast! But underneath . . .

"You didn't ask them specifically and they were not volunteering a single thing. For that matter neither are you. Which brings me to another point." Thatcher paused. "Captain, when I saw Yves Bisson's supplies of checks last night, they were on a table. Where did you find them?"

Ormsby smiled. "So you caught that, eh? You're absolutely right. They were both in his jacket. The forgeries on one side and the genuine checks on the other."

"No wonder he was so open about passing that check in Twin Forks. It was a simple error, and he didn't realize he was signing twice because of all the horseplay with the others. At least he didn't realize until the bus, when he pulled out the genuine ones that already had one signature."

"That's the way I figure it."

Thatcher was coming to a grim conclusion. "Well, that explains one aspect of the fraud that has been bothering me ever since Hathaway discovered it."

"You mean the timing?"

It was Thatcher's turn to be impressed. He had assumed that Ormsby was preoccupied with the murder to the exclusion of the Sloan's loss. "Exactly. In three days this whole world of Olympic Games will be blown to the four corners of the globe. Any criminal in his right mind would have arranged to pass that half-million in forgeries on the last day—and leave the police to cope with an exodus of over sixty thousand people."

"Sure. Until Yves Bisson's little mistake made it a whole new ball game," said Ormsby. "They knew he'd be picked up that night and his cache of forgeries with him. Once he was inside, he'd probably talk. At the very least, the bank would be warned. So his buddies decided to change the rules. They killed him and moved their whole schedule up. The really interesting question is how they found out."

Thatcher could not have put it better himself. "There are really only two possibilities. Either Bisson told his confederates himself after he realized his mistake—"

"Mr. Thatcher, with confederates like that, would you tell them?"

"Scarcely. So the overriding probability is that one confederate at least was present at Twin Forks and saw for himself. That certainly explains why one of your witnesses is lying."

Ormsby heaved himself to his feet. "It's some kettle

of fish. But there's one good thing from your point of view. It doesn't look as if the Sloan will have any more trouble."

"Yes, I think we can say the worst is over," said Thatcher, hitting an all-time record for one-hundred-and-eighty-degree error.

Thatcher's first act upon leaving Captain Ormsby was to check on the bank branch within Olympic Village, a scene of bustling normalcy. Thanks to yesterday's events, Sloan operations in Lake Placid were no longer profitable but at least they were being conducted with decorum and efficiency. It would be some balm to Everett Gabler to hear of the orderly lines, the swift transactions, the muted hum of computer equipment. Insensibly cheered, Thatcher continued on his rounds. En route to the downtown office of the Sloan his thoughts were much occupied with fraud and counterfeiting.

He never expected riot and mayhem.

And it is always the unexpected that paralyzes men. In the first dizzying moment after he opened the door, Thatcher actually thought the bank was under attack. Then he pulled himself together and realized that nobody was flourishing weapons. Even the great cacophony of shrieks and bellows filling the high-ceilinged room began to sort itself out. They were not, as Thatcher had first thought, eerie battle cries. He was simply listening to French as it is rarely heard outside of France. Finally individual vignettes took shape. There were two men who had slipped their hands beneath the grille and were trying to wrench it from its moorings, deaf to the entreaties of the teller on the other side. A woman in a chair was drumming her heels and keening hysterically while a man shouted at her.

Over by the desks, a small-loan officer had been seized by the lapels and was being shaken ferociously by a much larger adversary. Most startling of all was the sight of Roger Hathaway, backed into a corner with his arms raised defensively as a stout woman, her hair tumbling about her cheeks and her fingers curved into talons, made pass after pass at his face. She was impeded in her efforts by a frail bald man to her rear who had wrapped both arms about her waist and was desperately heaving backwards. Suddenly Thatcher spied an old friend, a bank guard borrowed from Exchange Place. He was hesitating halfway across the floor, his hand on his holster. Thatcher sympathized with his irresolution. Guards are trained to prevent holdups, not to save the bank manager from having his eyes scratched out.

"Hodgkins!" he bellowed. "Do you know what this is all about?"

Hodgkins made no effort to hide his relief. "Mr. Thatcher! Thank God you're here." He wiped his brow. "This is some kind of French tour group. It seems their money isn't any good. Do you want me to help Mr. Hathaway?"

Thatcher did not even spare the hapless manager a glance. "Nonsense, the man is a trained athlete. He can protect himself." He had registered the fact that treading warily amidst the carnage were a number of bona fide customers. "The first thing is to move this mess someplace else. Does this group have a leader?"

Hodgkins pointed. "I think that's him."

Thatcher's quarry did not look promising. He was standing by a counter, staring glassily into space and pounding his fist rhythmically.

"*Il ne manquait que ça,*" he said dully, over and over.

Briefly Thatcher wondered what the tour had been like until now. But he had no time for idle speculation. Instead he went to work and, within seconds, the leader was acting as stentorian interpreter. The announcement that the senior vice-president of the Sloan would see them all at his motel worked like magic.

By the time Thatcher had settled his thirty guests in the lobby—under the fulminating stare of the management—he had a very good general idea of the problem. The tour had left France the day before. Its itinerary called for three days at the Olympics, then on to New York for two weeks, followed by three days in Washington before the flight home. The first step for the group members that morning had been the attempt to provide themselves with American dollars. Under the new regulations prevailing in Lake Placid, they had been asked to wait during verification. As the Telex rapped out its dreary report, disappointment had reigned but, at first, there had been no move to violence. Then a member of the group had said casually that, if their checks had been stolen, Eurocheck would have to make good. A teller had incautiously replied that Eurocheck had no record of sales in their names. If Eurocheck hadn't sold them anything, it stood to reason that Eurocheck was not liable. That was when all hell had broken loose.

Now that calm had been restored, Thatcher was happy to see that many of the group members spoke English. They were using it, too.

"But what are we to do?" wailed a woman. "We are trapped in this terrible country without money. We will never be able to leave. We will starve to death. We will—"

Thatcher and the tour leader addressed themselves to allaying the worst of these fears. Transportation, hotel accommodations, two meals a day had already been paid for.

"Even the Olympic tickets," the leader said placatingly.

"What good are tickets now?" snarled one of his charges. "We are not going to see Bisson jump. I tell you it is all a plot against Yves Bisson. First they shoot him. Then they sabotage his tour."

Thatcher stiffened. "What is this about Yves Bisson?"

"We are all from Grenoble," explained the leader. "Bisson is one of our local men and we expected to see him take a gold medal."

Impatiently Thatcher waved this aside. "But what did he have to do with the tour?"

"It was *his* tour. You understand, he works for the travel agency in Grenoble that put this tour together, and he handled all the arrangements last summer."

"Exactly what arrangements were those?" Thatcher asked the leader.

"He did all the promotion, he made the reservations."

"And met with us," a woman sighed nostalgically. "In the flesh."

Privately Thatcher thought that was the least Bisson could have done for the people he was going to fleece. "And he arranged the purchase of the traveler's checks?"

"But of course."

Naturally. Bisson had simply pocketed the share of the payment intended for Eurochecks and supplied counterfeits. With the tour not arriving in Lake Placid until the concluding days of the Games, there had been little chance of his role being exposed.

But as Thatcher's gaze thoughtfully took in the distressed faces watching him, he decided not to repeat the folly of that teller at the bank. He would probably be lynched if he attacked the sainted memory of Yves Bisson. Let someone else do the dirty work.

"You will be relieved to hear that a representative of the French Ambassador is arriving here today to take charge of the body. No doubt you will be consulting with him, and I will certainly keep him abreast of any developments."

It was too much to hope that the Ambassador's representative would also be a proud son of Grenoble.

5 SOME FLURRIES

BACK in New York, Everett Gabler was indefatigably working his way down John Thatcher's list, despite one interruption after another. He had barely established that no other bank in the city had been troubled with counterfeit before the *New York Post* called, asking what he knew about thirty stranded Frenchmen. No sooner had he finished his last overseas call—this one to Eurocheck headquarters—than Walter Bowman arrived.

"Robichaux's here," he said. "Do you want to help me take him on?"

"I suppose," said Gabler rising, "it was only to be expected."

Robichaux & Devane, Investment Bankers, was an old and staid firm, whose association with the Sloan Trust Department went back a long way. Robichaux & Devane did the selling and the Sloan did the buying.

Tom Robichaux, with misplaced if touching guile, persisted in believing that he should try to seize the day.

Charlie Trinkam had another way of putting it. "While the cat's away, eh Tom?" he said genially, strolling in to reinforce Gabler and Walter Bowman.

Robichaux, who had the blue-eyed innocence of the very rich, deprecated the insinuation. "I only wish John were here," he said simply and untruthfully. "We've come up with some interesting situations—especially Zimmer Industries."

Zimmer Industries produced stony silence.

"Where is John anyway?" Robichaux asked, disappointed, as he always was, by the failure of his end run.

"Lake Placid," said Gabler, still braced.

"Good God, that's right!" Robichaux exclaimed. "The Sloan's involved with the Olympics, isn't it? My wife was reading about the trouble this morning at breakfast."

Tom Robichaux's wife, whoever she happened to be at the moment, was always a conversational problem. Walter Bowman, professionally swashbuckling, did not feel competent with non-stop marriage, divorce, alimony and remarriage. Gabler, naturally, had strong moral objections to Robichaux's hobby, which he regarded as particularly unsuitable in a banker. Only Charlie Trinkam, himself a ladies' man, was willing to venture a guess. "Oh yes," he said breezily. "The contessa."

For a confirmed bachelor, he had an enviable capacity to keep nearly current with Robichaux's hectic domestic progress.

"Contessina," said Robichaux in the interests of accuracy. "A contessina is the daughter of a contessa. Of course, none of these Italian titles . . ."

There were those who claimed that Tom Robichaux

never learned, his Quaker partner Francis Devane among them. This was not altogether true. Each wife, one way or another, broadened his horizons. Grazia's contribution was not, it developed, Papal titles or lesser Wittelsbachs'. It was, oddly enough, the Olympics.

"What was that you said?" asked Everett, who tended to close his ears when the subject was the reigning Mrs. Robichaux.

Robichaux was always willing to repeat himself. He —and the contessina, of course—had entertained Carlo Antonelli for a long weekend some weeks ago.

"He's Grazia's cousin," he explained. It did not occur to him to wonder why Gabler should care, so the matter of John Thatcher's list did not arise.

"What does he do?" he said blankly in response to Gabler's next question. "He's on the Italian bobsled team—"

"Yes, I know," said Gabler, startling Charlie and Walter Bowman. "But what does he do when he's not bobsledding?"

Robichaux blinked at him. "Things are different in Italy, you know," he said obliquely. "Carlo's family owns half of Cortina d'Ampezzo, as I understand it. He doesn't have to do anything—lucky devil. He travels a lot . . ."

It had taken massive efforts by the united Robichauxs to lever Tom, when he was Carlo Antonelli's age, into the family firm.

". . . knows how to enjoy himself. He brought a little French girl along who was a real honey," said Robichaux, with a connoisseur's smile. Then, sadly, "But it wasn't a success. For some reason or other, Grazia didn't take a shine to her."

Grazia, Charlie recalled, was a mature siren of riper

charms. He felt a sympathetic twinge of autumnal mel-
ancholy that was dissipated when Gabler said, "Would
you call him a playboy?"

Robichaux was beginning to look baffled so Charlie
hastily intervened. "A playboy who bobsleds, Ev. Now
about Zimmer Industries. . . ."

As Gabler marked time in New York, his many
calls were bearing fruit on two continents.

In Grenoble, Lucien Allard, owner of Voyages
Allard S.A., passed a trembling hand over his glisten-
ing brow. "All that is needed now to bring this disaster
to its ultimate completion is a miracle."

His companion, from the Banque de Grenoble, projected silent but ardent sympathy.

"If miracles did occur," Allard went on, "if Yves
Bisson were raised from the dead, I would kill him with
my bare hands. Thus to everything else, there would
be added mortal sin."

M. Allard was intemperate but M. Allard had cause.
He had risen to Bisson's murder with a florid elegy,
only to learn that the fallen hero was a not-so-petty
crook. Without faltering, he switched from tragedy to
treachery, concluding, as he had planned all along, that
life—*hélas*—must go on.

Then thirty-two Allard clients were stranded in the
wilderness!

". . . all their relatives, who believe that they are
without food and water. Also—much as I regret to say
so Air France is proving uncooperative, to say the least.
Naturally there are outcries from reporters—what do
you expect? But is it reasonable that the government
of France . . . ?"

This litany did not surprise the Banque de Grenoble.

Grenoble, normally a serene backwater, had been rocked by the happenings in Lake Placid—and no one more than M. Allard. But the Sloan had requested specifics, so the Banque de Grenoble was paying this little visit of condolence.

"Yves Bisson?" the banker murmured suggestively.

After the smoke of expletives cleared, M. Allard was forthcoming. A youthful, handsome athlete—what travel agent could not use him?

". . . to promote ski tours to Switzerland. You understand he had the glamour. Also, when Bisson himself traveled to a competition—well, here in Grenoble, people remembered that he was with the Voyages Allard. It made for the happy association."

But had Bisson really been a travel agent?

"Assuredly," said M. Allard with a mournful smile. "He sat there where you are sitting and told me he could not ski forever. He wished for a career after—a career where his name would be worth something. He wished to learn the business. Did I suspect he was a serpent? No, never. I said to myself, Ah hah! A hard head on young shoulders. But let him learn. I will teach him all the many complexities of a first-class travel agent."

In short (although that was not how Allard unburdened himself), Yves Bisson had worked industriously, learning the ropes for over a year. "No, not when he was skiing. . . . Yes, of course, we gave him time off. What else could we do? Publicity like that —superb!" But Bisson, between meets, had learned to route tourists, charter flights—and issue Eurochecks. He had had ample opportunity to make his nefarious substitution.

The Banque de Grenoble had more than one string

to its bow. There were also the police. A brief detour produced the salient facts. Bisson had had no known criminal associates. Like all young people, he was a familiar in the local discos and bars. But he was a young man to be proud of. It made one think, did it not?

Bisson's parents, prostrated by grief, were in seclusion in their apartment out in Marieville.

Wendell Lowder, Esq., lived in Denver, Colorado. He was the most important lawyer in the most important law firm in town, he was married to a cultivated wife, he had four wonderful children and he had traveled widely. But he lived in Denver and, beside this achievement, all else paled. In his cups, Wendell Lowder, Esq., could make relocation from Scarsdale sound like the Long March.

"Sure, out here in the West, we all know each other," he told the phone expansively. "Or if we don't, we just make a call. I got in touch with good old Floyd. Floyd's a trustee out at State—that's what we call Colorado State. About Dick Noyes. I've got it all scribbled down here somewhere. . . . Now let's see. According to Floyd, Dick's not much of a student. A C-plus average. But he's a damned good all-around kid—and one helluva skier. I can vouch for that myself. We've got a little place up in Aspen. . . . What? Oh, Noyes is a full-time student. No athletic scholarship or anything like that. His dad's a vet up in Steamboat Springs, and they're pretty well fixed. Summers, Floyd says he works for his dad. . . ."

In Garmisch-Partenkirchen the substance was much the same. The style, however, was different.

"It is most kind of you to see me on such short notice, Herr Rischler."

"My pleasure, Herr Kunstler. May I offer you some of the excellent coffee that my good Helga provides each morning at this hour?"

The cups were bone china.

This gavotte was not taking place in a tearoom but in the offices of the Mayor's Council. Herr Kunstler was visiting on behalf of the Association of German Exporters, a longtime Sloan account.

"You spoke earlier of an interest in Gunther Euler," said Herr Rischler, stirring delicately. "An outstanding young athlete, and one of whom our city"—he gazed blandly out his window at a forest of smokestacks—"is deeply proud."

"No doubt," said Herr Kunstler tonelessly. "But—and please correct me if I am in error—to be an athlete, unless one is rich, is sometimes difficult."

"Euler's father is a foreman in Klemperer's Foundry," said Rischler.

"Ah!"

There was a long pause during which Herr Kunstler composed his already composed features. "I am not myself conversant with the world of sports. But surely, for a poor boy, there are expenses. . . ."

"Traveling to meets and such things, you mean? Oh yes, there are expenses. They are met by donation from the West German Sports Confederation toward which the state—and the city of Garmisch-Partenkirchen, I am proud to add—make modest contributions. The bulk of such funds are raised from public subscriptions."

"Ah," said Herr Kunstler again. "My daughter is twelve years old."

Herr Rischler appeared to find this information engrossing.

"She is at the age where there are pictures from newspapers and magazines on the walls of her bedroom."

Herr Rischler waited.

"Singers with long hair. Strange wild-looking musicians," said Kunstler, a faint frown crossing his brow. "Her mother tells me there is a photograph also of Gunther Euler."

"A fine-looking young man," said Rischler.

"He is astride a costly motorcycle. Is that part of the expenses toward which you make the contribution of which you spoke?"

This time the *ah* was Rischler's. Then, with all the circumlocutions of which the language is capable, he dilated on how a poor boy who rose to athletic eminence might afford an expensive life style.

". . . a resort, you understand, which might feed and house him in great comfort. Then there are ski manufacturers who are delighted when Gunther Euler wins, wearing their equipment. I know nothing concrete, naturally, but that is the way these things are managed."

Herr Kunstler had an accountant's mind, with all its strengths and weaknesses. "But when he is not skiing, does young Euler work?"

"No," said Rischler. He was about to go on, then thought better of it. "No."

"So," said Kunstler, "his appearance of affluence can be explained. And it is difficult to see how Euler could be involved in an intricate system concerning counterfeit checks, is it not?"

To judge from Herr Rischler's expression it was difficult, but not impossible.

*   *   *

It was late at night before Gabler reported back to Lake Placid.

"Everett?" said Thatcher, after making sure that Brad Withers was out. "You're a good deed in an otherwise naughty world."

Gabler rightly disregarded this frivolity and proceeded. First he had to get Tom Robichaux and Zimmer Industries off his chest.

"Tom may have his faults," Thatcher replied, "but at least he doesn't have Olympic athletes on the brain."

"Now there's where you're wrong," said his loyal subordinate.

Thatcher listened to Gabler's haul for the day. It fleshed out his own impressions without materially altering them. Then his ear caught something.

"Is that all, Ev, or are you saving the best for last?"

Gabler did not know if it was the best; it was the only hint of anything useful to have come his way. "This Mathilde Lowengard," he began.

"Tilly," said Thatcher with a smile. He had a slight weakness for nut-brown girls.

"Miss Lowengard," said Gabler firmly, "lives in Wengen, Switzerland."

"Good," said Thatcher, recalling that lovely village clinging to the mountainside above Lauterbrunnen. "They don't allow automobiles in Wengen, you know."

"If Switzerland had an automotive industry, I am sure they would," said Gabler.

Thatcher tut-tutted. "You have no sentiment. Anyway, Tilly Lowengard lives in Wengen and . . . ?"

"And in the off season she works in Interlaken—in a bank."

If Everett expected a sensation, he was disappointed. "Since she's only twenty-one years old, I doubt if she occupies a highly responsible position. In fact, I suspect that Swiss banks find this a good way to subsidize amateur athletes."

"Highly unlikely," said Gabler. "A well-run bank has no business getting involved in foolishness of this kind."

"I'll tell Brad you said so," said John Thatcher.

6 NO RELIEF IN SIGHT

MEANWHILE, the Olympic pot was still bubbling away. Cross-country skiers passed one checkpoint after another; in the Arena, skating couples tangoed, waltzed and, in one case, hulaed; at all hours of the day and night vast throngs billowed in, through, and around Lake Placid. For most participants in this controlled pandemonium, Yves Bisson's murder was only one more event on the crowded schedule. Counterfeit traveler's checks drew less attention than the forthcoming hockey match between the U.S. and the U.S.S.R.

Not that everybody was concentrating on the public spectacle. There was a dissenting minority which included the thirty afflicted *Grenoblois,* currently deafening an unfortunate French consul. Also included, although less clamorous, were the New York State Police and John Thatcher.

"Yes, of course the Sloan will cooperate with whatever you have in mind, Captain Ormsby," he said, wondering why he had to reiterate the point. "Hathaway and I have excellent reasons for wanting to get to the bottom of this counterfeit scheme, don't we, Hathaway?"

If Roger Hathaway appreciated the united front, he was not sheltering behind it. "God knows I do," he muttered.

Thatcher made a mental note to take him aside for a pep talk, emphasizing the Sloan policy of standing by its own when it came to bad luck, as opposed to negligence. But he had to defer his morale building because Ormsby was still worrying the larger issue.

"Melville, the IOC, and a dozen ambassadors want to cooperate with the police, too," he said dispassionately. "Only, according to the governor's office, I've got to watch my step—not upset any arrangements, not bother any competitors. You get the picture?"

Thatcher did. "The Sloan does not expect kid-glove treatment. If it will help in any way, you can give Hathaway here a badge and swear him in."

This mild pleasantry did not, as intended, improve the atmosphere in Hathaway's small office.

"He's the man I want," said Ormsby. "Or at least I think so."

Thatcher sympathized with the fleeting uneasiness he caught on Hathaway's face. "Yes?" he said cautiously.

"I asked you down here because I figured we'd have to have your okay, Mr. Thatcher," Ormsby explained. "But what I want from Hathaway is a list of the names on all the Sloan counterfeit."

With or without Thatcher's approval, this was a taller order than Ormsby knew and Hathaway said so: "Oh, my God!"

Before Ormsby could misinterpret, Thatcher softened this response: "We can compile those names for you, but what will it tell you?"

"I don't know," said Ormsby, "but we can start with

the names that are members of the Olympic family. Bisson was a competitor. He lived in Olympic Village. The way I look at it, the place to begin is close to home."

"Yes indeed," Thatcher murmured. He did not add that the task force arriving from the Sloan was not going to stop there.

Ormsby's exercise swung into operation immediately. By dawn the following morning, Roger Hathaway, still red-eyed from six hours with stacks of worthless scrip, found himself cast in a leading role.

Flourishing his credentials under the security guard's nose, he loped through the lobby of Olympic Village toward the auditorium. Captain Ormsby and John Thatcher were there before him. Otherwise the room was deserted.

"Good," Ormsby grunted, sweeping Hathaway into his briefing session without delay. "Now, once you gave me that list, Hathaway, we got to work. Out of all the people who passed counterfeit, nearly a hundred were Olympic competitors or coaches. In other words, people right here in Olympic Village. We're going to interview every single one of them, and we're going to do it today."

His plan was simple and drastic. The police had posted Olympic Village with a wanted list. Between seven in the morning and seven at night, everyone on it was to present himself in the auditorium.

"That gives them plenty of time to go do their stuff," said Ormsby. "But when they get back, they report here—or else!"

"Don't let the silence mislead you, Hathaway," Thatcher advised. "Beyond these four walls, all hell is breaking loose."

Hathaway could guess. Protests from coaches, howls from national committees, fulminations from sportswriters, must be reverberating outside, mingling with thunder from the IOC.

"We'll run them in and out like clockwork," said Ormsby calmly.

Looking around, Roger began to see the bare bones of the system. A uniformed policeman and a secretary were just taking up stations at the long table near the entrance. "They'll check off the names as people turn up," Ormsby explained. "And if they don't turn up by seven tonight, we go out and get them."

Halfway down the auditorium was another table where the staff was still assembling. All of them were in uniform.

"They check on where everybody was day before yesterday, when Bisson was shot. We still don't know how the counterfeit meshes with the murder. For all I know, the murderer didn't touch any counterfeit himself, let alone pass it. But it won't do any harm to ask."

Taking his cue from Thatcher, Hathaway remained quiet.

"And here's where you come in," said Ormsby, pointing to a nearby table.

"Oh?" said Hathaway with resignation.

"I've volunteered on your behalf," Thatcher said, leading him across the auditorium while Ormsby conferred with a subordinate. "No doubt you hoped for time off after your efforts last night, but I'm afraid that's going to have to wait."

Disregarding the niceties, Hathaway asked what he was supposed to do.

There were written instructions. Assisted by a secretary, Hathaway was going to focus on Eurochecks. Where had they been bought, and in what denominations? How many counterfeits had been passed—and how many remained? How securely had they been kept? How accurately had they been recorded?

". . . and anything else you can think of," Thatcher concluded. "I don't have to tell you that, if you get a hint of anything suspicious, you alert Ormsby or me. We'll be around this morning. The reason you've drawn this chore is that, presumably, you're more sophisticated about European banks than Ormsby's staff—and, we hope, than the people you'll be interviewing. Double-check the issuing banks and institutions and, if any of them rings false, let me know."

"Everything but the kitchen sink," Hathaway commented, still reading.

Thatcher eyed him. "Among lawyers, fishing expeditions have a bad name, Hathaway. But bankers find them useful and so, I gather, do the police."

"Sure," said Hathaway, but by then Thatcher was gone, disappearing out the door with Captain Ormsby.

Hathaway sat down to wait. An hour later, he was still waiting. Eight o'clock came and went, without a single Olympian, and Captain Ormsby's tight organization began to fray slightly. Policemen tilted chairs back, stood up, stretched. The secretaries took to disappearing, then returning with cups of coffee. From somewhere ashtrays appeared, and the spit and polish of preparation gradually collapsed under the untidy litter of routine. Still no clients appeared.

"Say, this must be a nice change for you, getting to work here in Lake Placid instead of New York City."

Roger, who had almost dozed off, came thumping back to reality. A large, rosy-cheeked trooper had ambled over, all innocent friendliness.

"It's great," Roger replied.

"Of course, this isn't the real Lake Placid," said the

trooper, settling on a corner of Hathaway's table. "You should see it once everything gets back to normal."

The sooner Roger saw the last of Lake Placid, the better. His unencouraging silence did not make a dent.

"Is the Sloan staying open here?"

"We close two weeks after the Olympics shut down," said Roger, wondering how often he had produced this answer.

"How about that!" marveled his visitor. "Is that your job—opening and closing temporaries?"

"This is just an assignment," said Hathaway.

But Trooper Bork had the persistence of a puppy. "My sister works for a bank, too. She's a teller over in Burlington."

The past twenty-four hours had been no picnic for Hathaway. Fortunately, before he could tell this guardian of law and order to go jump into Lake Champlain —and take his sister with him—there was a halloo from across the room.

"Looks like we've got some business," said Bork, shoving off. "See you around, Rog."

But like everybody else in the auditorium, Hathaway had shifted his attention to the first fish scooped up in Ormsby's net. A quartet of Dutch skaters, dismayed to discover they were ahead of the field, hesitated in the doorway, unwilling to advance or retreat.

"Come right on in," coaxed the nearest officer, nearly defeating his purpose. Finally a tall, straw-haired boy gulped and advanced. Ten minutes later he was still apprehensive.

"We're from the Sloan and we've got a few questions about your traveler's checks," Hathaway began. "Your name is . . . ?"

"Conrad van Teutem," the boy replied while the secretary, Olivia, downed her coffee and consulted a list.

Conrad van Teutem had exchanged two hundred and fifty dollars, purportedly issued by the Eurocheck office in London, but in fact counterfeit. His remaining checks, which he surrendered with reluctance, were all genuine.

"Thank God!" he exclaimed ingenuously. "With that money, I am going to tour California."

"You'll love it," said Olivia warmly.

Roger Hathaway was not interested in California. "Why London?" he asked, recalling Thatcher's instructions. "Why didn't you buy your traveler's checks in Holland?"

Van Teutem, stuffing the precious folder in his pocket, looked up. "Because I live in London. I explained it all to them, to the police. My father is with KLM."

"I lived in London for four or five years," said Hathaway, suddenly wishing he could turn back the clock.

Young van Teutem was not responsive. In his short life he had already lived in Athens, Djakarta and Moscow. Furthermore, he preferred snow-swept wildernesses to any city.

"I guess that's about all I've got to ask you," said Hathaway, unaccountably irritated. When van Teutem left, he exclaimed: "God, what a waste of time this is!"

Everything but blow drying her hair was a waste of time to Olivia. "I suppose so," she said indifferently.

Just then a second Dutchman presented himself. Since he lived in Utrecht, not London, Hathaway put him through his paces without any further distractions.

For the next two hours, he was too busy for nostalgia or for regret. After the Dutch came a trickle, if not a deluge. Singly and in groups Olympians began turning up. At times they stood on line, at times they proceeded without delay. But anxious, affronted or excited, they completed the circuit with Hathaway and his battery of questions. Inevitably, several oddities came to light. A surprising number of athletes, like Conrad van Teutem, did not live in the countries they represented. Chileans resided, trained and bought traveler's checks in Frankfurt. Italians gave Swedish addresses.

"No, I don't think there's anything wrong with it," said Hathaway to a sputtering, Zurich-based Finn. "I'm just making a note—that's all."

"Also," said the Finn with a roll of his eyes, "you say three hundred dollars of counterfeit. Impossible! I am too poor. Only one hundred dollars have I changed since I am here. I show you."

He thrust a thick folder of genuine Eurochecks at Hathaway, together with meticulously kept dockets. "Well?" he demanded.

"I guess it's just that your records don't tally with ours," said Roger, unwilling to debate the point.

"I am not rich," said the Finn, despite his cash on hand.

He was not the first to challenge Olivia's list with a plea of poverty. The cult of the simple life loomed large at Olympic Village, and so did a hazy disdain for numbers.

Gunther Euler was the exception that proved the rule.

"Seventeen thousand dollars," said Hathaway, returning Euler's Eurochecks. "You're carrying quite a roll, aren't you?"

Olivia, meanwhile, was fluttering her eyelashes.

Euler enjoyed their reaction but he had an explanation ready. "After the Olympics I go on to Japan.

For that, there will be big expenses. So, I am prepared."

"Uh huh," said Hathaway, although he was representing the Sloan Guaranty Trust, not the Olympic credentials committee. "Well, they're all okay. And you say you don't have any idea how this counterfeit you passed turned up? How much was it, Olivia?"

"Six hundred dollars," she said admiringly.

Euler did not like Hathaway's tone, but there was nothing defensive about him. "Doesn't everybody know? Poor Yves must have put them in my wallet."

A lion, twitching his tail in the sun, could not have been more superb. The posture impressed Olivia, but it left Hathaway feeling his years. "Okay, Gunther," he said dismissively. "Thanks for the cooperation. And good luck in the combined jump."

But he was destined to see more of Gunther Euler before the day was out.

After dealing with an English figure skater, a Rumanian hockey coach and another Dutch speed skater, Hathaway awoke to a room-wide stirring. One of Ormsby's men was just closing the door.

"We're breaking for lunch," Olivia informed the girl approaching them. "You'd better come back later."

Miss Tilly Lowengard, however, was firm. "This afternoon I am racing. I cannot come back later," she said, plunking herself down defiantly.

"All right," Hathaway said absently. "This shouldn't take too much time. You can go on ahead, Olivia. Now Miss Lowengard, I've got a few questions. . . ."

He wheeled them past her, mechanically noting down answers. ". . . Bank of Interlaken? . . . Now, according to our records, you passed a hundred and fifty dollars in counterfeit—"

"No!" she burst out. "All my checks were legitimate.

That I am certain of. I myself saw Herr Dangler issue them. You see, I work in the bank, so I know."

He recalled his wandering attention. "Oh, do you? Well, let me take a look at your remaining checks."

But while he riffled through them, Tilly continued her impetuous protest. "And since I work in a bank, I am always careful. When I sign a check, I make a very careful record. They say that Yves must have placed a counterfeit, but that is not possible."

"Maybe in all the excitement you slipped up," Hathaway suggested, as he had suggested before.

"No," she said stubbornly.

He repressed a sigh. There was no sign of Ormsby or Thatcher, and a few more minutes of seepage from the room would leave him sitting there alone. He rose. "Well, I'll put that down, Tilly. You don't know what happened." To keep her from pursuing her quarrel, he went on: "We appreciate your cooperation, too. Now, I think I'll go over to the cafeteria to grab a sandwich."

"I will come with you," she declared, as he had guessed that she would. The mulish glint in Tilly's eyes was not lost on Hathaway. She still had plenty to say. And, all things considered, he should probably hear her out.

But with his ham on rye came a breather.

Dick Noyes spotted them as they stood, trays in hand, searching for a place to roost. "Hey, Tilly!" he yodeled, rising and waving. "Over here! What are you doing here? Aren't you racing this afternoon?"

"Tea only," she said, threading her way toward his table. "And some toast. Do you know Mr. Roger Hathaway from the Sloan?"

"Hi," said Noyes incuriously. "Tea? I always load up with steak and potatoes on the days I'm competing."

"Me, too," said Gunther Euler, with a cool nod toward Hathaway. He cleared a space for Tilly's tray on the littered table. "Even on days when I only go out to practice, like today."

Tilly grinned. "I have already eaten my steak and potatoes, at breakfast. What do you do this afternoon, Dick?"

"What do you think?" he replied with a grimace. "I've got to go talk to the police again. But then I'm heading out to Whiteface, Tilly, to watch you break every record in the book."

His buoyancy did not mask a flicker of constraint, barely noticeable in the cheerful hubbub of the cafeteria. This particular trio, Hathaway suddenly realized, shared special links.

Then, with grave courtesy, Noyes turned to him. "Do you get a chance to catch many of the events, or are you too busy, Roger?"

"Not as many as I'd like," said Hathaway. "It's been a disappointment. When I went over to Innsbruck—"

"You were at Innsbruck?" Euler interjected with studied insolence. "So was I!"

"The whole world knows that, Gunther," said Tilly gaily. "This is my first Olympics."

"Mine, too," Noyes chimed in.

Their conversation swirled on, leaving Hathaway odd man out until Noyes remembered his manners again. "Do you ski, Roger?"

"A little," said Hathaway modestly. "I used to ski for Dartmouth."

"Great," said Noyes. "Listen, Tilly, I'll see you at Whiteface but I've got to beat it now."

"Yes, good luck, Tilly," said Euler, ignoring Dartmouth completely.

Hathaway watched them march out of the cafeteria with mixed emotions. Turning, he found Tilly frowning darkly.

"I must go, too," she said. "But before I go . . ."

He forced himself to face the fact that there was more work for him to do.

7 OCCLUDED FRONT

BEYOND the cafeteria steam tables were the Olympic Village kitchens. Beyond them were storerooms, piled high with everything from sardines to sourdough. And beyond that was a barnlike area with overhead doors opening onto a receiving dock.

Twenty minutes later, at just about the time that Roger Hathaway was following Tilly Lowengard out of the cafeteria, John Thatcher found himself surveying two giant trucks backed against the platform. A work gang was unloading them with rhythmic efficiency.

"Miss Maas? She's in the office with the invoices," one of them replied to Ormsby. Then, shifting a crate of grapefruit, he loosed a bellow that echoed through the chamber. "Katarina! Visitors!"

A long-legged girl with a mane of tawny blond hair came through a side door. She was wearing a white shop coat and carrying a sheaf of papers. Her business-like appearance was marred, however, by the man at her side. He was just slipping his arm from her waist.

"Hello, Vaux," said Ormsby shortly. "I didn't expect to see you here."

"How could you, when I merely stopped by to learn if a special shipment for my team has arrived?" Vaux turned to Katarina Maas. "You'll let me know when it comes?"

"Of course," she said, brushing by him. "How can I help you, Captain?"

After that, it was no surprise to have her repeat Vaux's story almost word for word. Their encounter on the bus had been accidental. They had stopped at the motel on a whim. Their walk at Twin Forks had been inspired by scenic beauty.

As Thatcher observed her, he had to admit that her manner gave some support to Ormsby's earlier suspicions. She was certainly still under thirty, but the sleekness of her grooming and her self-assurance set her light years apart from the contestants like Tilly Lowengard. There was a casual arrogance in her femininity that suggested she took what she wanted—and no unknown Madame Vaux back in France would stop her.

Thatcher awoke to the realization that Miss Maas was finally departing from her companion's script.

"Yes, I noticed that it was Yves Bisson who paid for the rental," she was saying. "He had to persuade the man to accept a Eurocheck."

"Oh?" Ormsby grunted. "Vaux claimed he was too far away to see what was going on."

"That is not surprising," she replied, unruffled. "François was talking with the Deladier girl so we were momentarily separated." Suddenly her calm evaporated. "And it was all such childishness. Yves was simply rubbing it into Gunther that he had placed first and he was likely to win the gold medal. It's not as if those snowmobiles are cheap. There was no reason why the others shouldn't have paid their share. And Carlo Antonelli is a rich man."

It was strange how Yves Bisson's generosity had exasperated so many people. Dick Noyes, Thatcher recalled, had still been protesting.

"Surely it could have been a straightforward song of triumph by Bisson," Thatcher suggested. "Without any wish to cause pinpricks."

Katarina Maas tossed her head. "Even so, it was still a folly. But these athletes, they are all suffering from the same disease."

"And what is that?"

"Arrested development," she said icily. "You only have to look at them. Take Tilly Lowengard."

Even Ormsby caviled at that. "What's wrong with her? She seems like a normal, healthy girl."

"Normal!" Katarina's laugh was so mocking that it caused two workmen to drop a carton and look nervously across the room. "Do you call it normal for a grown woman to behave like a ten-year-old boy obsessed with his model railroad? Do you realize that, for years, her every waking moment has been concentrated on shaving one second from the women's slalom record? Every personal habit has been tailored to that end. And for what? There's no future in it. Even if she succeeds, what will happen? Two years from now, everyone will have forgotten her. She'll simply be a twenty-five-year-old woman who's missed out on everything. I don't understand her at all."

Thatcher could readily believe it. "You think Tilly Lowengard and Suzanne Deladier are perpetual juveniles?"

The wide grey eyes never blinked. "I was only talking about Tilly. There's nothing wrong with the way

Suzanne's head is screwed on. Surely you have noticed the difference between women skiers and women skaters. Why, if Suzanne wins the gold medal, she'll be snapped up by one of the ice shows, she'll get a long-term advertising contract, there will be personal appearances, maybe even a movie career like Sonia Henie."

She stopped, relishing the vision she had created.

"Then you'd say Miss Deladier views her years of training as an investment on which there will be a return?" Thatcher asked.

But these terms were more congenial to a banker than to Katarina Maas. "Myself, I would call it a gamble," she corrected him. "And why not? Long shots have paid off before. After all, nobody expected Suzanne to win the French Open, and she did. Maybe the same thing will happen here. But that is why she does not participate in the immature games of the others. That is why she does not spend her time running around with some handsome boy on the French team. She may look like an ice maiden, but she has the mind of an adult."

Before Katarina could continue, she was hailed by the unloading crew.

"I must check out this delivery so the truck can leave," she explained. "If you have further questions, would you ask them while I work?"

Captain Philip Ormsby was not the man to be deflected by her obvious desire that they leave. Strolling in her wake, he continued to put his questions as she industriously ticked off items on her invoices. Miss Maas was uniformly unhelpful.

She knew nothing about Eurochecks. She herself had a personal account in New York.

"At the Chase Manhattan," she amplified for Thatcher's benefit.

She had no idea how well François Vaux had known Yves Bisson. She herself had never met any of the Olympic participants until last week. They were virtual strangers.

"You seem to have taken the measure of Tilly Lowengard and Suzanne Deladier," Ormsby pointed out.

"I know something of the women because I lodge in their dormitory," she explained coolly. "I rarely see any of the men contestants."

The outing to Twin Forks had been an exception. Normally she was too busy to take time off.

"As you can see," she said, waving off the first truck and preparing to deal with the second.

"Yes, indeed," said Thatcher, whose attention had been engaged by the diverse goods spilling into the warehouse. Boxes of dried herring and crates of cabbage had followed hard on the heels of cases of ketchup and bottles of pickles. "It must be incredibly difficult, catering to so many nationalities."

Immediately she was all business. "Oh, this is nothing compared to the Summer Games. With so many Asians and Africans, they have to take into account widely varying diets and religious interdictions. But here there's no problem like that. Everybody is working hard outdoors in a cold climate. So they all want a high protein diet. Beef and chicken are our mainstays. Of course there are national differences in the side dishes. Almost all the coaches have some sort of special shipments for their teams. The French get cheeses and the Scandinavians get fish balls. But at least your American officials are cooperative. I hear that in Sapporo, the customs held up some German sausages until after the games. I haven't had any trouble like that."

She was a different woman when she was speaking about her job, so much so that she was almost cordial as she said good-by in the midst of the bustle of a freshly arrived load of caviar for the Russians.

As they made their way through a brightly clad crowd of skiers in the parking lot, Ormsby was thoughtful.

"For a girl who didn't want to tell us anything, she gave me plenty to think about," he said finally. "Take Suzanne Deladier. If she's honestly hoping to make herself into a millionaire here in Lake Placid, then this is the last place she'd choose to get involved in a criminal caper."

"It would scarcely be worth her while," Thatcher agreed. "But I was more interested in what Katarina Maas was unconsciously telling us about herself. Did you notice how she assumes that all motives and returns are financial? I would say that Miss Maas goes through life looking for a fast buck."

Ormsby steered them toward his police vehicle that was almost the only sedan in the lot, dwarfed by the surrounding buses and trucks. "Talking of Katarina, what did you think of that little scene with Vaux that we were supposed to have interrupted? For a man trying to hide an affair, he's taking a lot of chances."

"He was trying to hide it before he became a suspect in murder and grand larceny. It might be the lesser evil now," said Thatcher, studiously fair. "But I agree that today was a put-up job. There were signs all over Olympic Village announcing the arrival of the police and the Sloan to discuss Eurochecks. Vaux knew we'd see him. What I don't understand is why he's shoving his relationship with Katarina down our throats."

Ormsby revved the motor contemptuously. "He's no more having an affair with her than I am."

"It was your idea," Thatcher reminded him.

"That's because I was day-dreaming. I must have temporarily lost my marbles. The Twin Forks motel has been fully booked for over a year. You know what the situation is. The Lake Placid area doesn't have enough hotel rooms for sixty thousand tourists, let alone enough roads for their cars. So they've established a thirty-five-mile area into which no private cars are allowed. That's why we're the only Ford around," he said with a wave at the towering eminences rolling along the road ahead of them. "Most of the tourists are staying outside the circle and get bused in. Anyone who's got a room inside has got something rarer than a seat for the Muhammed Ali fight. I don't know why Vaux took the Maas woman to that motel but it sure wasn't to shack up." He was struck by a sudden notion. "In fact, you can say that in this entire circle nobody is taking anybody to a motel room to play house."

Thatcher was amused. "This must be the only thirty-five-mile area in America about which you can say that."

"Only for twelve days," Ormsby grinned. "Then it'll be back to normal."

"Which leaves us still wondering what those two are up to."

After a moment's hesitation, Ormsby decided to share some private information. "You know we've had the wires busy checking into these people's background. Nobody's got a police record, but Vaux comes the closest. When he did his military service, they didn't care for the way he handled the funds on some sports spectacular he organized. They eased him out instead of giving him a court martial, but it was a near miss. The trouble is, that makes him out to be a petty crook, not the kind who's got the contacts or the stomach for international fraud."

While reminding himself to tell Everett Gabler that his sources were not infallible, Thatcher decided that he could share insights, if not information.

"You know, when I saw Miss Maas receipting those invoices and when I took in the volume of deliveries, I couldn't help realizing that there was a setup made to order for her. A supplier could short-weight his shipments and give her a kickback. Unfortunately that doesn't leave any role for Coach Vaux."

Ormsby was interested. "How much do you think she could get away with before the shortages were self-evident?"

Thatcher had too much experience with this kind of situation. "Probably around two thousand dollars a day."

"Forget it. I know the food wholesaler who's got the Olympic contract. That kind of chicken feed wouldn't be worth it to him." Ormsby gave his companion a challenging look. "You bankers are all alike. You think in terms of fraud and embezzlement and kickbacks. I move in different circles. There, when you want to steal something, you just take it. You don't bother shuffling a lot of papers."

Thatcher had to admit there was a good deal of justice in Ormsby's accusation. Thatcher did habitually think in terms of white collar crime—of crooked books and fictitious payees.

"You mean why should Katarina be content with a kickback? Why shouldn't she simply insist on full deliveries and then make off with two thousand dollars' worth? Well, you've just stated the obstacle—transport. How is she going to get away with ten sides of beef?

She can't drive out of the area with them, and she can scarcely take them on the shuttle bus with her."

Ormsby was now smiling broadly. "I know, I know. But I wanted to remind you of the facts of life."

"I take it there's nothing in her background to support this."

"Nothing along those lines. But there's something that might interest you. This is a new job for her. She used to work for Lufthansa. Two years in Germany and then two years in the New York office."

Thatcher was ashamed of his first reaction. "So that explains the New York bank account."

"She got to you with that, uh?"

Thatcher rose above parochialism. "But you're right, it opens up all sorts of avenues. With that history, Miss Maas could have contacts in travel agencies and Eurocheck outlets all over Europe."

"It's a cinch she's up to something with that boy friend of hers. But it's going to take time to find out what."

"Time," Thatcher repeated as they pulled up on the town's main street. "That's just what we don't have. Another forty-eight hours and the Games will be over. Then all these people will disappear over the horizon."

Ormsby heaved himself onto the sidewalk and carefully proceeded to lock the car. "I wouldn't be too sure of that, Thatcher. I have high hopes of getting that deadline extended."

Thatcher had listened too long to Brad Withers on the subject of the sanctity of Olympic schedules.

"If you have any thoughts of persuading the IOC to elongate its activities, I can disabuse you, Ormsby."

"They may not have the final word." Ormsby was almost smug. "I was thinking of higher authority."

For a dizzy minute Thatcher could see ambassadors

and prime ministers summoned into play. Then he realized that the police captain was standing stock still, staring expectantly at the sky.

"Planning on heavenly intervention?" Thatcher asked sarcastically.

"More or less." Ormsby beamed. "I was on to the weather station this morning. They've already got two feet in Buffalo and it's moving this way. The forecasters are talking about the blizzard of the century."

With a valedictory wave, he headed for the police station.

8 SNOW JOB

THATCHER hesitated a moment too long on the sidewalk outside Town Hall.

"John, just the man I'm looking for!"

Brad Withers was striding across the street, his rubicund face glowing with anticipation. The Sloan's president, Thatcher thought resignedly, was probably its only employee who could view the situation in Lake Placid with undiminished enthusiasm. Even the tellers, according to Roger Hathaway, were taking the half-million-dollar rip-off to heart. But Withers had weightier problems on his mind.

"It seems we're in for a little snow," he announced.

"I had heard that."

"Grand, isn't it?" said Brad, taking a deep breath and expelling a cloud of whitish vapor.

Thatcher wondered if Ormsby and Withers had listened to the same forecast. Ormsby was expecting a killer blizzard. Brad seemed to be thinking of a gentle dusting.

"I suppose the weather might raise a few problems," Thatcher suggested.

"Nothing to worry about. But I agree with Melville that we should offer our counsel to the local people. I'm on my way there now. The only trouble is, I can't be in two places at once."

Thatcher refrained from asking why a town that made its living as a ski resort needed guidance on snow removal. He was more concerned with what was coming.

"No, you can't," he agreed, avoiding any rash offers of assistance.

Brad looked at his senior vice-president trustingly. "You see, we make a point of having an IOC member present at every event. That way, the youngsters know we're taking an interest. And I was supposed to be at the women's slalom this afternoon."

It could have been a lot worse. Thatcher hastily offered to pinch-hit before Withers could think of some less palatable form of service. The slalom was always an exciting spectacle, and it certainly beat scheduling overtime for snowplow crews.

By the time he was in an IOC car being driven to his destination, he realized that he had been too cavalier about the problems facing the local authorities. This was Thatcher's first trip along the narrow twisting road that led to Whiteface Mountain where the downhill events were taking place. During the nine-mile course he saw two buses, going in opposite directions, barely brushing by each other. On one side of the road there were the rocky outcroppings of the Adirondacks; on the other side there was a tumble into the brawling mountain stream they were following. There was no room at all for maneuver. Losing even a foot of road width would present difficulties. And overhead the sky was growing blacker and blacker. Not surprisingly, Captain Ormsby's expectations were beginning to look a good deal more reasonable than Brad Withers'.

But the weather had not affected attendance. As soon as Thatcher left his limousine, he was reduced to just one more body in the crowd good-naturedly pushing its way from the parking lot. Most of them were heading for the lifts that serviced the different stages of the ascent up the mountain. They filled the air with knowledgeable comments about various vantage points. Thatcher trailed indecisively in their wake, wondering where a deputy IOC official should take up his stance. A sudden greeting spared him the necessity of making a choice.

"Mr. Thatcher! Have you come to watch Tilly win it?"

Dick Noyes was making no secret of his partisanship. And he knew exactly where they should site themselves.

"Follow me," he urged, heading for a chair lift, "and you'll be able to see the last set of gates and the finish line—even in this murk."

"I'm surprised you can spare the time," Thatcher remarked, trudging after his guide. "Shouldn't you be practicing for your own race?"

Noyes grinned. "For a deputy IOC member, you haven't been keeping up," he charged. "My event was over yesterday."

His tone of voice gave Thatcher no clue as to the outcome.

"How did you do, or shouldn't I ask?"

The grin broadened. "I placed thirty-fifth in a field of thirty-six. That's pretty much where I expected to finish, but I could have done without Gunther Euler's crack. He congratulated me on finding someone in the world I could beat."

Thatcher agreed that there was no need to rub salt into wounds.

"Oh, I can see his point of view," Noyes said tolerantly. "Gunther doesn't think much of college boys fooling around with skiing only as long as they're in school. He even got off a couple of snide remarks about Roger Hathaway."

"He prefers a more professional approach?"

"Watch it! That's a dirty word around here," Noyes warned in mock alarm. "Everybody knows how the IOC feels about amateurism. Some of them would like nothing beter than to dig up a stinking scandal in the Winter Games."

Thatcher cast his mind back over the last few days. "If that's what they want, surely they have it," he said with some heat. "Or don't murder and forgery count?"

"That's not the kind of scandal I meant," Noyes began, as they were landed at Mid Station. "Hey, Carlo! Over here!"

Carlo Antonelli's style was more urbane. He delayed his response until he was within conversational range. Then he explained that, as the bobsled run was occupied, he had decided to watch the slalom.

"They tell me that your Tilly has a good chance," he concluded.

"She sure does. You know, Tilly placed second in the European Women's Championship and Helga Mueller is out with a broken leg." Suddenly Noyes sobered. "Poor kid! She did it over at Killington two weeks ago. Fibular injuries are no joke and hers is a complex fracture. She'll miss two seasons at least."

For a moment Thatcher was startled by the judicious gravity. Then he remembered Everett Gabler's report.

Of course the boy was in veterinary school and knew all about fractures. In fact, Thatcher decided, he had almost been guilty of the same mistake Katarina Maas had made in her indictment of the financial innocence of Olympic athletes. There were all sorts of economic realities besides the rewards of a gold medal, and people blind to one could be alert to another. Dick Noyes, happily bouncing around the Olympics, probably knew all about the value of a beef herd, all about the average income of a livestock veterinarian. And Carlo Antonelli was not a mindless playboy either. He probably had the dollar figures of resort operation at his fingertips. After all, how many people meeting Tom Robichaux in a nightclub would guess that he spent his daylight hours trying to unload stock in Zimmer Industries? What it boiled down to was simple. Commercial ventures came in many guises—including the wholesale counterfeiting of traveler's checks.

This meditation was interrupted by a crackling from the PA system and a roar gradually descending the slope.

"They've started," cried Noyes.

Carlo Antonelli glanced at the lowering sky.

"And not a moment too soon," he said. "In five minutes we won't be able to see anything at all."

Watching the first three women contestants was undiluted pleasure for Thatcher. He had always enjoyed the spectacle of experts at work, even when the physical manifestation was as pedestrian as an auditor checking a ledger. But here, coupled to the precision of turning, was the excitement of speed and the grace of skis carving the snow as surely as a baker frosting a cake. He was so absorbed he did not even notice the first flakes as they began to fall.

The fourth starter was Tilly Lowengard. From the

moment her name was announced, Dick Noyes made such a racket that Thatcher was barely able to hear anything else. He was dimly conscious of the usual chorus of yells from above, the constant shifting of spectators seeking a better view, the crackling of the announcer. Left to his own devices, he would have suspected nothing. But he was standing between two competitors who carried their own internal stop watches.

Dick Noyes stopped dead in the middle of one of his encouraging war cries and cocked his head.

"What's going on?" he asked uneasily. "She's terribly uneven. You can tell by the way they're shouting at the gates."

"They've been shouting all along," Thatcher said.

Noyes brushed the remark aside impatiently. "There's a different quality when she passes by them. She's been fast and then slow and then fast."

Antonelli agreed with him. "Maybe it's the snow," he offered without much conviction. "It's thickening up. Maybe the track is changing."

Thatcher refused to join fruitless speculation. "Well, whatever it is, we'll see in a minute."

The words were barely out of his mouth when Tilly appeared around the turn.

"Something's wrong!" Noyes cried.

Even to Thatcher that much was clear. Tilly was all over the place, her skis splayed, her balance maintained only by her plunging sticks. Her first swing was so wide that she was actually canted along the side wall, her second was so tight that she clipped the gate. With one ski in the air, her belated attempt to straighten seemed doomed.

"She's out of control, she's going to crash," Noyes moaned.

But with a desperate heave Tilly delayed the inevitable long enough to skid ingloriously across the finish line. There, stewards and judges scuttled hastily out to her erratic path. Still speeding, she headed toward a knot of bystanders, managed to jump-turn at the last moment, then failed to recover. With one tip dragging disastrously, she buckled up, slammed into a snow bank, and the run was finally over.

Fortunately, before Dick Noyes could do much damage to the spectators he was manhandling aside, Tilly began struggling to her feet.

"She's not hurt," Thatcher and Antonelli said simultaneously.

But it was the sight of the Swiss coach and the stewards hurrying forward, rather than his companions' words, that halted Noyes' impetuous rush.

"I guess Tilly wouldn't thank me for stampeding out there," he said, reminding himself of Olympic niceties.

Antonelli answered with the frankness of an old hand. "She certainly would not. Her performance was bad enough. Leave her what dignity she has left. Anyway, she's all right. Look, she's walking under her own power."

For the onlookers, the suspense was over as soon as they saw Tilly groggily weave her way off the field, surrounded by a cloud of attendants. For Tilly the ordeal was just beginning.

"Where are we going?" she asked, conscious of a hand steering her away from an inviting bench. "I want to sit down."

"You have to go to the Medical Center to be checked out."

"There's nothing wrong with me," she protested. "I got shaken up, that's all."

"It's just a precaution," said a detestably persistent voice.

Tilly had enough experience with crashes to diagnose her own complaints. She would be black and blue all over tomorrow. Her painful left shoulder was merely suffering from a minor wrench. No bones were broken.

None of these facts explained her languid disassociation from the scene of which she was the center. Why did all sounds appear muffled and far away? Why did everyday objects keep going out of focus? For that matter, what were the Swiss coach and the stewards arguing about so heatedly over her head? For the moment Tilly simply did not care. She wanted to sit down, to lean back, to close her eyes.

Not until she was decanted from the first-aid truck at the Medical Center did she consider the possibility of concussion. But she had been wearing a helmet throughout her run, it was still in place, and she could not remember hitting her head against anything harder than snow. All these thoughts she presented, in disjointed phrases, to the doctor who poked and prodded, then grunted as he came to her shoulder. Throughout the routine of X-rays and ophthalmoscopes, Tilly grew more detached, hearing directives only when they had been repeated several times, then often misunderstanding them. The world had shrunk to a series of meaningless imperatives:

"Bend your knee!"

"Don't close your eyes!"

"Tell me when the lines cross!"

Then, like a burst of machine gun fire, two words penetrated the fog.

"Urine sample!" she repeated with something approaching her usual energy. "What are you trying to say?"

An Olympic athlete would have to be dead before he failed to recognize the implications of this phrase.

"You think I'm taking drugs," Tilly raved. "Well, you're crazy! I've never taken an amphetamine in my life."

But the period of lucidity blurred under the onslaught of official voices cajoling, ordering, reasoning. They were citing regulations, urging her not to take offense, advising her to prove her innocence.

Then the face of the Swiss coach swam into focus.

"Tell them they're wrong, Wolfgang," she pleaded.

"Under the circumstances," he replied stiffly, "I have agreed they are justified."

There followed the whole humiliating procedure of the little cubicle, the jar, the label affixed by a white-coated technician, the lofty pretense that this was a normal medical test. Normal! Tilly shivered to think of the consequences of a positive result. Disqualification, expulsion from the Olympics, disgrace!

"You'll see," she warned them, very close to tears. "And you'll apologize."

"Perhaps," the doctor said unsympathetically, "but you'd better go now. The tests take more than an hour, and there's an American boy waiting for you outside."

"To hell with American boys!" snapped Tilly. She could see that the doctor had already made up his mind. Did he think that competition skiers drugged themselves to do worse than usual? "I'm not budging until the results come through. I'm staying right here."

The doctor shrugged. "For the time being," he said ominously.

An hour later he not only had the results, he had a

speech ready for delivery to the delinquent. He was in full flight as he entered the waiting room.

"There is no longer any question. You have only yourself to thank for this situation, but it would have been pleasanter for both of us if you had received this notification through your team manager. . . ." He stopped when he realized that his words were being wasted on empty air.

Tilly Lowengard was sound asleep.

The ordeal had not ended for John Thatcher either. He had forgotten his semi-official capacity until the stewards sought him out. As Dick Noyes was standing by his side during the explanations, Thatcher's first duty became tamping down an incipient explosion. He did not delude himself that he had succeeded. It was Carlo Antonelli's happy suggestion that Dick's place was by Tilly's side which had prevented an assault on the officials.

Then Thatcher had returned to the motel with a budget of bad news for Brad Withers.

"I'm afraid the women's slalom can be regarded as a shambles, Brad," he reported. "The stewards canceled after only five runs. The snow's so thick up there, the skiers can't see where they're going."

"But that will upset the whole schedule," Withers objected.

Thatcher had formed his own opinion about the forthcoming schedule during the thrilling ride back from Whiteface Mountain.

"What's more," he continued remorselessly, "the judges have demanded a urine sample from one of the competitors. They're convinced she was skiing under the influence of drugs."

"Good God! Think of the publicity that's going to

cause!" Brad exclaimed. "We'll have to tell Melville right away."

"*You'll* have to tell him," Thatcher corrected. "Hathaway just called. The Sloan has dispatched five people to trace back those fake traveler's checks, and I have to get the procedure organized."

Brad Withers' incomprehension proved one thing, Thatcher decided. Dick Noyes had been right. In the eyes of the IOC, there was only one kind of scandal worthy of the name.

9 COLD CANADIAN AIR

THE first sound to penetrate Thatcher's sleep-clogged brain the next morning was the voice of Brad Withers.

"Good Lord, where did you get an idea like that? Of course I'm all right."

There was a back-to-the-wall exasperation in these remarks that could only mean he was speaking with his wife. One fact regularly threatened the harmony of Brad's home life. Whenever it became necessary to breach his ivory tower with news of the real world, the unwelcome messenger was almost always Mrs. Caroline Withers.

Blinking drowsily, Thatcher strolled into the living room of their suite to discover that his guess was right. Brad, wrapped in yards of Sulka silk, was pacing the floor while he clutched the telephone with a strangulation grip.

"For heaven's sake, Carrie, have you gone crazy? . . . I don't know what's gotten into you. . . . Naturally we're going ahead as planned. . . . Good-by!"

Slamming down the receiver, he was gratified to find an audience at hand. Thatcher had sunk into a chair and was flicking on the news.

"Women!" Brad fumed. "They can't seem to understand what's important and what isn't. Carrie expects us to call off the Olympics because of a little snow. Where does she think we should hold the Winter Games? In Florida?"

His final snort was almost drowned out as the television set came to life.

". . . whiteouts of exceptional ferocity throughout our viewing area. State Police in northern New York and Vermont have closed all major thoroughfares. Only rescue vehicles are being permitted on the roads as the hunt for stranded motorists continues. A state of emergency has been declared in the cities of Plattsburg and Burlington, and authorities urge everyone to stay indoors until the storm eases. Medical hotlines have been established for those requiring hospitalization. The number to call in New York State is . . ."

At least, thought Thatcher with relief, that explained why he felt he was living underwater. Those thick muffling curtains were on the outside of the windows, not the inside.

"I believe we're in the middle of what they call a whiteout, Brad," he began cautiously. Now was certainly not the time to explain that a suspension of Olympic activities might operate in the interests of the Sloan Guaranty Trust. "It means that there's no visibility and—"

"I know what a blizzard is like," Brad grumbled. "It's simply saving us the trouble of using the snowmaking equipment on the downhill runs. If only people wouldn't try to blow up a simple problem—"

103

Before he could continue his denunciation of all those people he happened to be married to, the phone was once again luring him into an unwelcome dialogue. This time it was the head of the IOC, and his opening remarks were enough to turn Brad into a tower of outrage.

"Cancel!" he cried. "Look here, Melville, I can't go along with that. This isn't some high school basketball game, this is the Olympics!"

The reply did not make things any better.

"You've already made the announcement!" A touch of hauteur became evident. "Well I must say, Melville, that's prety high-handed."

As the conversation progressed, Thatcher found it hard not to sympathize with the acting president of the IOC. If his call had only come first, Brad might have been reasonable. But with that strange perversity which invests all marital struggles, Brad now regarded any concession to Melville as a point scored for Carrie. Under these circumstances he was ready to argue until doomsday. Only the introduction of a new subject moderated his stiffness.

"I don't see much point to a conference as you've gone ahead on your own," he concluded, still huffy. "But if you want to talk about that girl, too, then I'll come. And what's more, I'll bring Thatcher with me. He's met her and he'll be able to tell us about her."

Little as Thatcher cared for being presented to the IOC as an intimate of the Olympics' most recent drug imbiber, he realized as they marched down the long corridor that he was in the enviable position of having something to do. From every door came the static-riddled voice of a newscaster; at regular intervals there were knots of disconsolate residents lamenting the vital tasks going unperformed because of the storm.

In Suite 301 they found the plenipotentiaries of the Olympic Games in full array. Brad was inspired to remark, "No wonder we're all on time. We're all under the same roof."

"If we weren't all staying in the same motel, we couldn't be having this conference," Anthony Melville snapped back instantly.

He sounded like a bear at stake. It was no surprise to learn others were deploring his early morning announcement.

"In order to have a conference, it is necessary to confer," said a legalistic German. "How can we confer about a decision that has already been taken—and implemented?"

"For God's sake, what was there to confer about?" demanded Melville. "I'm not talking about a matter of judgment. I'm talking about a matter of physical impossibility."

The jabber of voices was deafening.

"Listen to me!" Melville glared them all down. "In the first place, the engineers on Whiteface say the downhill runs won't be usable for two days. The cables and the pylons for the lifts are iced over, they've got steady winds of sixty miles an hour with gusts up to ninety, and nobody's even tried to measure the drifting. Second, the traffic supervisor says there's no hope of opening the road to Olympic Village before nightfall." He swallowed painfully before continuing. "And, if you must know, the network people called me at six o'clock this morning. They can't transmit up to commercial standards."

There was an appalled silence. ABC's purchase of

television rights was all that made the Olympics financially feasible. But it was well known that Anthony Melville, a lifelong foe of commercialism in sports, preferred to ignore that unpalatable fact.

The Japanese delegate rescued them. Returning to fundamentals, he said, "So, it is exactly as you have stated. This is a matter of physical impossibility."

"And now that we have that cleared up, perhaps we could go on to the next point," Melville said gruffly. "I have here the official medical report certifying the presence of a foreign substance in the urine sample from Mathilde Lowengard. She's the Swiss girl who put on that shameful performance yesterday. I assume we're unanimous on withdrawing her accreditation. If so, we'll notify the head of the Swiss delegation that she's to be expelled."

The Swiss at the end of the table coughed. "In principle I agree. But I understand that Miss Lowengard is very popular and claims that there are extenuating circumstances. Therefore—"

"If the girl is popular and influential, that makes her conduct even more outrageous!"

"I agree, I agree. It is not the girl I am thinking of, but her teammates. They are shocked and disturbed. I would not like them to think we had acted summarily. If we could explain the situation to them . . ."

"The IOC does not speak with mere athletes." Melville was shocked.

"But surely these are exceptional circumstances. The team is so upset that a number of the contestants are threatening to leave in sympathy. What if they all go?"

Melville made a mighty effort to sound reasonable. "Now look, Schoenburg, we've faced this situation before and the same thing always happens. The trouble lasts only as long as the transgressor is here. We ship him out, he goes home and gets a hero's welcome, and everybody in Olympic Village forgets about him as soon as the next world record is broken. We've got a tried-and-true method that works, and I say we should stick with it."

"I am not quarreling with the decision, merely with the way it is announced," Schoenburg said doggedly. "Perhaps there is another way to sugarcoat the pill. Instead of the team, what if you met with the head of the Swiss delegation?"

A thin triumphant smile appeared. "Impossible. Because he's in Olympic Village and there's no way to get there. And this is certainly not a subject I care to discuss on the phone. No, we'll follow our standard procedure. My secretary will call his secretary, relaying our decision and demanding that Mathilde Lowengard be expelled forthwith."

This imperial fiat remained unchallenged for all of ten seconds.

"How?"

Taken by surprise, Melville swung around almost threateningly. He had been so intent on his dispute with the Swiss that he was baffled by this intervention.

"What do you mean by that?" he growled.

The Japanese stood his ground. "If there is no way into Olympic Village, then there is no way out. How is Miss Lowengard to be expelled?"

Thatcher appreciated the struggle reflected on Melville's features. What the acting head of the IOC wanted to say was all too clear. But he was not completely blind to the forces of publicity. Already he could see the cartoon that would appear in every major capital of the world—Tilly Lowengard wrapped in a shawl with her bundle of shame, Melville as the stern father pointing into the stormy night, the immortal phrase floating overhead: *Never darken my doorway again.*

Melville took a deep breath. "Naturally when I said forthwith, I meant with all reasonable dispatch. As soon as the roads are open, she has to go." But the concession had been so painful he could not forego one last ill-advised comment. "This is what comes of continuing with the Winter Games. They're infected with commercialism and we'd be better off without them."

Battle was joined instantly.

Norway and Sweden—both with strong contenders in the women's slalom—had been noticeably silent in the cause of Tilly Lowengard. Now they rushed into the fray to support Switzerland and Austria. None of these countries could field the teams necessary to make an impression in the Summer Games, but in the Winter Games they could challenge even the superpowers.

On the other side of the table new alliances were also forming. Brad Withers and Melville shared a devotion to the ideals of amateurism. According to Melville, his opponents made shameless use of the Games to promote sports industries important to their national economies. Brad contented himself with a paean to the purity of the Summer Games, studded with references to personal acquaintances and confined rigorously to the equestrian and yachting events.

Under cover of one particularly vigorous broadside, Mr. Hayakawa moved up the table and dropped into the seat beside Thatcher. He wore a puzzled frown.

"Did I understand Mr. Melville correctly?" he inquired. "Is he maintaining that the Soviet ski team is a band of state hirelings while their field and track team is composed of dedicated amateurs?"

"That's what he said," Thatcher agreed, "but only in the heat of the moment."

"He'll be lucky if there are any Summer Games this year."

Curiously enough it was Brad Withers who returned them all to the problem at hand.

"Say what you will about the Summer Games," he declared roundly, "at least we've never had to postpone them because of a blizzard."

"Yes, and look where that leaves us," said one of his supporters. "We've got Tilly Lowengard still at the Village, and all the contestants penned up with nothing to do but listen to her grievances. And furthermore this may go on for days."

Melville was more relaxed now that he had let off steam. "Things may not be that bad," he said, returning to his role as chairman. "The traffic supervisor has been talking to the weather station. The snow is going to continue through tomorrow, but the wind is due to drop. If it does, they can at least open the road from the Village to the town. Now I have a suggestion. One of the events scheduled for today was the Short Program of the women's figure skating. That takes place indoors and the network wasn't going to carry it anyway. So, always provided the road can be opened, I say that we hold the competition and throw it open to the entire Olympic family. That will break up the siege condition at the Village, help us lighten the post-blizzard agenda, and give everyone someplace to meet and something to watch."

The advantages of this proposal were so manifest that it seemed it would pass by popular acclaim. Then one voice was raised in dissent. It was the legalistic German again.

"But what about the tickets for the Short Program? Most spectators who bought them won't be able to get to the Arena tonight."

Given the Great Ticket Debacle already swirling around the Town Hall, this refinement brought down the house.

10 VIOLENT ELECTRICAL STORMS

MRS. Carrie Withers was not the only one impelled to the telephone by the weather. Whenever airplanes drop feed to cattle in Wyoming, whenever twisters scythe through Kansas, whenever eggs fry on the sidewalks of Minneapolis, AT&T knows about it.

True, winter was hitting the whole eastern third of the United States hard. But a disproportionate share of the world's media was already at the Olympics. Most of the inevitable pictures of cars nosing into snowdrifts, roofs dotting a white ocean, plows laboring around the clock, originated in Lake Placid. This set off a rush for the dial tone around the world.

In Manhattan, Miss Corsa was taking twenty-seven inches of snow in stride. "But Mr. Lancer"—the Sloan's Chairman of the Board—"wants to be sure we can contact you during the emergency," she explained.

And why wasn't George C. Lancer calling himself?

"Because when he got through last, he was stranded at a Howard Johnson's on the Massachusetts Turnpike," Miss Corsa reported sedately.

It was an entertaining vision but Thatcher did not linger over it. "What's the rest of the damage?" he asked.

Apart from branches closed from Syosset to Harlem, loan officers marooned in the wilds of Westchester, and visiting dignitaries bunking down in various executive offices (including Thatcher's), the Sloan was doing as well as could be expected.

"In fact, this weather isn't all bad, John," said a new voice. Charlie Trinkam had unceremoniously dealt himself into the conversation. "Washington's closed down tighter than a drum, the Open Market meeting's been scrapped, and Henry Kauffman's plane has been diverted to Atlanta. We haven't heard anything nutty about interest rates for twenty-four hours."

With this, their exchange became heavily technical until one of Trinkam's contentions made Thatcher ask, "What does Gabler think about that?"

"You know Ev," said Trinkam, telling Thatcher all he needed to know.

"No doubt you and he and the Investment Committee will work it out," said Thatcher.

"You bet," said Charlie ambiguously. "And how are things in Lake Placid?"

Rightly assuming that Charlie was not interested in snowfall data, Thatcher cast around for the *mot juste.*

"Confused."

"Nobody's turned up with a confession in one hand and a half-million dollars in the other? Say, that reminds me. I'd better be getting along. I was just on my way down to Quarles. He's on the warpath. If Ev runs into him before I do, we're going to have blood in the corridor."

With this Trinkam departed, leaving Thatcher considerably mystified. Quarles was the Sloan's chief cashier. He had superb technical qualifications and nothing whatsoever to do with policy making.

"Why should he be gunning for Gabler?" Thatcher asked Miss Corsa, who had been patiently standing by. "I may have been away too long, but I don't see why he and Gabler interacted at all."

"It's because of the storm," Miss Corsa explained, resisting the temptation to embroider Thatcher's truancy. "All of our departments are shorthanded. I understand that Mr. Quarles is upset at losing four of his most experienced people."

This, Thatcher realized, represented a severe pruning of a luxuriantly tangled grapevine. Normally he respected Miss Corsa's reticence. But he wanted to get to the bottom of this.

"Exactly what does Gabler have to do with four of Quarles' most experienced people?" he demanded implacably.

"Why, Mr. Gabler sent them to Lake Placid," she said, as if he should have remembered.

"Ah, yes," he murmured, just as another thought struck. "I hope they're not snowbound somewhere around Albany!"

"Oh no, Mr. Thatcher," she assured him. "They arrived late last night. They're staying at the Andiron Inn, if you want to contact them. They were only supposed to be away for a day or two, but now there's no telling when they'll be able to get back."

Thatcher ignored the reproach in her voice. "Well, it won't be time wasted. With luck, they'll do the Sloan more good here in Lake Placid than they could in New York."

Mr. Quarles did not look at it that way. Neither did Miss Corsa.

*   *   *

London called too.

G. Withers Austin, Bradford Withers' nephew, was an ornament of the Sloan branch there. During his busy day, he invariably found time for many newspapers and magazines. Today's reading struck a chord, and not much later he was talking to Lake Placid.

"Well, Roger, how's life in the Arctic Circle?"

Wind was rattling the storefront windows of the Sloan. On his own initiative, Hathaway had ordered most of the tellers to stay at the Andiron Inn. He and three other veteran skiers had fought their way downtown, then shoveled open the branches. The bank on Main Street was officially doing business for the very few customers who struggled in, with demons howling each time the door opened. When the door closed, the CB scanner took over: ". . . roads impassable . . . electrical outages . . . missing bus . . ."

"Who is this talking?" he demanded.

"Bud," said G. Withers Austin, hurt.

"Bud?" Hathaway repeated. Then, at the last possible moment, light dawned. "You mean Bud Austin? Well, for God's sake! What are you doing back here?"

Bud Austin, as someone had unkindly observed, was one of the happy ones. "No, no, I'm still here in London," he chortled, "thanking my lucky stars that Nancy and I didn't decide to take in the Olympics. We were tempted, let me tell you. Remember what a good time we all had at Innsbruck? Nancy was talking about it just the other day."

"Me, too," said Hathaway, recalling Gunther Euler.

Inadvertently he flustered Austin into apologetic half-sentences: "Hell, I keep forgetting . . . the way things turn out . . . anyway, Nancy decided . . ."

Resigned, Hathaway let the prattle flow on. There was no way, he knew, that he could reassure Bud that

the divorce had left no deep scars, even when Molly
remarried. If Hathaway missed the golden days when
the young Austins and the young Hathaways had London and Europe at their feet, it was only because he
was so far out of the magic circle now.

". . . always thought you and Molly had a really
solid marriage," Bud was saying earnestly. "So did
Nancy."

It was impossible to dislike Bud Austin. Nancy was
something else again.

"What's Molly's new husband like?" Hathaway asked
unkindly.

Bud was pained. "He seems nice enough," he said
reluctantly. "We met them when they came over last
fall. He's got a ranch somewhere in Arizona."

"With Molly's trust fund, I'll bet he does," said
Hathaway—to himself.

Austin, who had his share of the family dignity, got
back on track. "Anyway, Roger, I've been meaning to
call you even before this blizzard. You've been having
a little trouble with counterfeit at Lake Placid, haven't
you?"

"We've had half a million dollars' worth of counterfeit, Bud," Hathaway replied. "I'm staying at a dump
outside of town where everybody's had to double
up because we've got bank investigators coming out
our ears. Plus the police—and others when they can get
in. A little trouble isn't the way I'd describe it."

"It sounds hellish," said Austin.

"It is."

"The reason I bring it up is that we were circularized
by New York the other day. I told myself to call you
and get the real dirt."

This was news to Hathaway. In the tumult of sub-
sequent events, he had forgotten Everett Gabler and

whatever he was doing in New York. For the first time, he visualized circles rippling out from Captain Ormsby in Olympic Village all the way to London. "I wonder why," he said slowly. "We didn't get stuck with fake British pounds. I suppose it could be the foreign currencies that were issued in London—"

"That's it," said Austin. "We're running around to every foreign bank here. But, and this is good, New York wants to know about counterfeiters in the British Isles. Can you picture Strachan's face?"

"Bud, from where I sit, this is no laughing matter," Hathaway said. "This blizzard is the final straw. It's going to stop, sooner or later, but I've got a lousy feeling that heads are going to roll—starting with yours truly."

Bud Austin had virtues as well as defects. "Don't talk like that, Roger. As soon as you get away from Lake Placid, things will start looking up. And don't forget, I can always put in a good word for you with Uncle Brad."

"Thanks, Bud," said Hathaway. "I appreciate that. But I wonder if that's going to be enough."

Cortina d'Ampezzo spoke to Lake Placid, New York, as one winter resort to another. In both of them, snow was white gold.

"But there can be too much of a good thing," said Carlo Antonelli's mother, keeping a sharp eye on her diamond-studded watch. The Antonellis could well afford any transatlantic charges they wanted, but they were not making foolish gifts to the telephone company. "And it could not have come at a worse time. How much longer will you have to stay there?"

"Who knows?" he replied. "At the moment, the

weather is bad, very bad. Conditions for skiing or sledding . . ."

She could picture the insouciant shrug, and she knew just what to make of it. "Do not pretend that you don't care, Carlo," she said. "Even before this delay, there was too much strain."

"Yes, mama," he said with mock filial docility.

"And this is no time to make jokes!" she retorted. Signora Antonelli was one of those rare creatures, a woman worthy of her couturier clothes. Despite her willowy elegance, her glowing skin and her deep chestnut hair, she disliked being told that she looked more like Carlo's sister than his mother.

"Here, let me talk to him," said Franco Antonelli. Bald and tubby, he was half a head shorter than both his wife and his son. "Carlo, are you there?"

"There is no place I can go, papa," said his son with affectionate irony. "The snow is piled high."

"Your mother and I have been very worried about you, and about the whole situation," said Antonelli senior.

"Franco," said his wife with a worried frown, "be careful! You do not know who may be listening."

"We did not like this fantastic scheme from the very beginning," Signor Antonelli continued. "You know that. But there was no reasoning with you. Now, however, the question is, can you get out of this without a tremendous scandal? I do not want to see our name in headlines, Carlo."

"What can I do?" Carlo rejoined. "Who expected policemen everywhere? It is bad luck that everything has become so difficult. By now the Olympics should have been finished. Could I know that they were going to drag on and on?"

"Yes, yes," said Franco Antonelli, rolling his eyes at his wife. "Well, now it cannot be more than a matter of days. No doubt the newspapers exaggerate. Surely they will start rescheduling—"

"As a matter of fact, the Arena events are continuing," his son interjected. "There will be figure skating tonight."

"Why didn't you say so!" Franco crowed joyfully. "Mafalda, they are going on with the figure skating. That means the end is in sight!"

"Oh, Carlo!" she cooed, snatching the telephone.

He rejected these waves of pleasure. "Who knows what can still happen at Lake Placid?" he asked morosely. "Maybe they will ask us to stay after the Games are over. If that happens, I do not know what I can do!"

His father, as usual, had the last word. "Now Carlo, be a man. You got yourself into this predicament. Let us only hope that God will get you out of it. You know that we are waiting for you eagerly—and that you have all our love." Then, embarrassed by this outpouring, he recovered himself. "But I hope you realize that it is time for you to grow up. You are too old to play games like these. Everything is amusing to you, Carlo. Too amusing. As you are discovering, it is well to be very serious about life."

"Believe me, papa, I have ceased being amused."

There was one more call, this one from Plattsburg.

"Listen, it's now or never. . . . What do you mean, the weather? . . . What could be better? Everybody's out working like hell, or they're staying inside. It'll be clear sailing. . . . What? Of course I know how to do it. . . ."

11 THIN ICE

ANTHONY Melville, one-time gold-medal archer, retired hanging judge from Vancouver, B.C., and acting
president of the International Olympic Committee, was
devoid of romance. Nevertheless, when his program
came to pass that evening, the women's figure skating
provided one of the magic moments of the 1980 Winter
Olympics.

Under heavy snow, road crews toiled throughout the
afternoon to open a single lane of the highway from
Lake Placid to Olympic Village. By evening, a cautious
convoy began ferrying the contestants into town. Other
than that, Lake Placid was isolated from the outside
world, transported back to an age innocent of organized spectaculars. Instead of diesel fumes, there was
clean white snow, falling, falling, falling. Instead of an
ear-shattering din, there was the silence of nature
arched over the clamor of man. As darkness fell, lights
winked on creating an impromptu *ville lumière,* with
fantastic shapes outdoors and comfort and cheer within. Hurrying from motel to restaurant, from bus to

coffee bar was exhilarating, not terrifying. Bitter cold remained, but the wind had died down and gradually more and more young people arrived. The exuberant American hockey team, fresh from last night's victory over the U.S.S.R., walked all the way. Insensibly, the air of festival grew.

Contrary to his expectations, John Thatcher found himself in the midst of it. On disentangling himself from the telephone, he had become aware of a certain restlessness. He did not know whether to attribute it to Charlie Trinkam's jaunty allusions to doings in New York, to the continuing impasse here in Lake Placid, or to simple cabin fever. But whatever the cause, a long walk was called for and Thatcher was soon striding up Main Street. A solitary stroll through the woods would have been preferable, but bottomless drifts ruled this out. It was plowed streets or nothing, and Thatcher found plenty of company besides rambunctious young athletes filling the air with snowballs.

Several elderly couples, muffled to the chin, were walking besweatered poodles. Groups of children cavorted under the watchful eyes of golden retrievers and Newfoundlands. One decorative couple promenaded stylishly behind three Old English sheepdogs.

Scattered over the idyllic scene, however, were knots of frenetic activity and Thatcher came on one just outside Town Hall. A jeep, wreathing exhaust fumes, was being loaded by a crew drafted from their Olympic desks.

"Food," one of them grunted when Thatcher inquired. "There are hundreds of visitors stuck in those motels where they don't have eating facilities."

Thatcher, watching a case of dried milk disappear into the hold, was reminded of his friends from Grenoble. The crew knew all about them.

"The Northland Motel," said the driver bitterly. "Last trip but one. Remember, Jack?"

"How could I ever forget?" Jack asked. "Thirty Frenchmen and two pregnant women. If you want my opinion, people should pray quietly—not at the top of their lungs."

Thatcher left them to their chores. Hardship, he reflected, was taking on new dimensions for Yves Bisson's hapless compatriots. Proceeding, he encountered Roger Hathaway letting himself out of the bank.

"Yes, we opened today—a little late, but we opened," he said.

"Congratulations," said Thatcher. "Apparently, the same cannot be said for many of our Long Island branches. Of course, we do not hand pick the personnel there for athletic ability. Tell me, how are conditions up at the Andiron Inn?"

Hathaway had not been expecting the conversation to take this tack. "Fine," he said blankly.

"Enough food?" Thatcher pressed.

Hathaway cast around. "Food's no problem. We are running a little short of bed space since these guys from New York landed. But on the whole, everything's fine."

Thatcher asked about the progress being made by Quarles' delegation.

"None," said Hathaway with the ghost of a smile. "They couldn't manage to get down here to the bank today. But fair's fair. They didn't come prepared. We're scouring Lake Placid right now for a pair of size 13EE boots."

Since Thatcher could think of no appropriate comment, they strolled on in silence. After a while, however, it became apparent that Hathaway was progressing with a sense of purpose.

"Heading for the figure skating?" Thatcher asked.

"Only incidentally," Hathaway replied. "I'm trying to track down Ralph Beeman—and I might be able to catch him at the Arena. He's in charge of Olympic maintenance and equipment. He told me this morning that they hadn't sent anybody out to Hoevenberg or Whiteface yet. I want to find out how the situation looks now."

When Thatcher did not immediately take him up on this, he explained. "Even when the weather lifts, grooming for the outdoor events will take time. I'd like some sort of working estimate on how much longer the Games are going to last—so I can plan."

This, of course, made good sense to Thatcher. Once the Olympic Games were over, the process of dismantling the Lake Placid Sloan would commence. But, under the circumstances, this was a case of locking the barn door with a vengeance. There was no way that Hathaway could bring this particular project in under budget. So Thatcher said, "Well, I think I will look in on the skating. Why don't you join me?"

It was hard to tell whether Hathaway welcomed this invitation or not, but he dutifully changed course and in a few minutes they reached the rink. It was a vast oval, glowing opalescently under artful illumination. At the far end, a judging panel sat strung out in straight-backed chairs, studying every move made by the slim figure at center ice. Along the sides, limbering up or toweling perspiration away, were other slim figures, surrounded by retinues. Beyond, in semidarkness, were the onlookers. They did not fill the Arena to capacity, Thatcher saw, as he and Hathaway hesitated at the top of an aisle. But there were enough spectators to make a sizable crowd, buzzing with enthusiasm and, occasionally, flowing over into noisy cheers.

"Good heavens," said Thatcher, following Hathaway to a seat, "I hadn't realized that the Olympic family was so big. In theory, they're the only ones who could get in tonight, aren't they?"

"There are nearly two thousand out in the Village," Hathaway said. "And add to that the television people, the Olympic staff, and all the sponsors."

"And most of them are here tonight," Thatcher concluded. Anthony Melville had been right. An unusually strong and pleasing sense of camaraderie created a feeling of real community.

For a while, they sat in silence, watching spins, pirouettes, and double-axle leaps.

"Do you know who this skater is?" Thatcher asked.

Hathaway squinted at the board but, before he could reply, an outburst from several rows ahead answered Thatcher's question for him. The young lady was Czechoslovakian.

Thereafter, the announcer identified succeeding skaters and Thatcher watched them with a banker's interest. Here, if Katarina Maas was to be believed, was where the money was.

"Oh, I don't know," said Hathaway, when this was put to him. "Sure, that used to be true. But things have changed. Nowadays it isn't a matter of glamour events versus nonglamour events. Almost all of these kids have a shot at making real careers for themselves out of the Olympics."

"Go on," Thatcher encouraged him.

"Oh, I don't say that the bobsledders have much riding for them, but as for the rest of them—well, look at Jean-Claude Killy. He's done as well, if not better, than most figure skaters."

"That's true," said Thatcher. "Yves Bisson was trading on his name at a travel agency, wasn't he?"

Hathaway preferred to keep the conversation general. "In Europe, a big-name skier is like a rock star, complete with groupies. They do pretty well out of their amateur status. And if they play their cards right, they can parlay it into big things."

Thatcher found himself thinking of Tilly Lowengard. But before he could formulate a question, a great tumult broke loose. "What is it?" he yelled above the roar.

Voices in every imaginable language told him. Vera Darskaya from the U.S.S.R. had just taken an impressive lead. And barely was she off the ice than the announcer, with a tremor of excitement, boomed the name of the final contestant: "For France, Suzanne Deladier."

From where Thatcher sat she looked unbelievably vulnerable.

12 DISCOMFORT INDEX

TEN minutes later found John Thatcher again congratulating Anthony Melville. Suzanne Deladier's performance was something he would never forget. It was physical perfection, succeeding physical perfection. But what set it apart, Thatcher realized as he watched, was the special quality of this particular audience. Like the public, these spectators oohed and ahed. There was applause, critical attention, rapture. Yet the atmosphere was unlike anything Thatcher had encountered at previous Olympic events. There was a sense of intimacy in the vast skating rink. Suzanne Deladier was not a person apart, performing and entertaining. Somehow everybody was skating with her, sharing her effort. They knew, as no other audience could, what she was doing. For one breathless moment, the contest element faded. They were all together, linked by the Olympic spirit of athletics for the sake of excellence and nothing else.

This, it soon developed, was the last empyrean interlude Thatcher was destined to enjoy for the rest of the evening. Almost immediately he was pitched willy-nilly into a roller coaster of sensations.

Thatcher, on his feet and cheering like everybody else, felt an urgent hand on his elbow. Turning, he encountered Bradford Withers.

"That was a splendid performance, wasn't it?"

"This time," said his chief with dark emphasis and an unmistakable waft of brandy. "This time I'm not taking no for an answer, John. Come on!"

Implementing this show of force, he dragged Thatcher into the aisle and began propelling him toward the exit. Thatcher had no alternative but to let himself be towed away with nothing but the briefest nod over his shoulder to Hathaway.

Detaching Withers was not the problem. The brandy was. Alcohol in Withers' bloodstream raised unpredictability to toxic levels.

"Where are we going, Brad?" he asked, as they cleaved through the crowd.

Withers was astonished he had to ask. "Why, to the disco, of course!"

"Of course," said Thatcher hollowly.

Discos are discos, on Thirty-third Street, in Peoria or in Olympic Village. Blackness stabbed with crazy-house lights . . . tribal frenzy and individual trance . . . a giant pulse of music flaming and inflaming, clutching and releasing, filling reality.

John Thatcher perched on an inadequate wire chair as near the exit as he could get. He accepted the need for disco in the modern world. War, pestilence and fever exist. Why not disco?

He was alone. Withers had disappeared in the lemming run from the minivan into Olympic Village. Possibly he was somewhere out there in that jungle tangle.

If so, let him look out for himself. There were limits to the risks that Thatcher was prepared to take.

"Mr. Thatcher, may we join you?"

Carlo Antonelli stood over him, arm in arm with Katarina Maas. Thatcher, for want of anything better to do, studied them. Antonelli wore a turtleneck and ski pants. Miss Maas sported an exiguous silver lamé frock with infinitesimal straps. Both of them glowed with a faint sheen.

"Please do," he said, rising. Never had he felt more like a port in a storm.

"I am afraid not," said Miss Maas unapologetically. "Now, I must go."

She caught Antonelli unawares. "Go?" he repeated, a wire chair dangling unheeded from one hand. "But the party is just beginning."

Even without a clipboard, Katarina Maas was crisp. "For you athletes, for the dignitaries, it is a party. For me, it is work. I have been here since six o'clock, arranging the buffet."

Thatcher was growing bored with Olympic logistics. "I thought there was a non-stop disco here in Olympic Village, Miss Maas. Why has this caused you extra work?"

"Because," she said, her cool superiority totally unruffled, "our discos are for the residents of Olympic Village. Mr. Melville insisted that we throw open the doors to everyone in Lake Placid who was able to come. Now, I must bid you good evening."

Antonelli chuckled as she disappeared into the darkness. "The displeasure is aimed at me, not you," he explained. "Miss Maas is dismissing an unsatisfactory courtier."

"How have you offended?" Thatcher asked curiously.

"It was not difficult. That one expects to be treated

like a queen. I merely suggested, after one dance with her, that we sit the next one out. She chose to interpret that as a criticism."

"And was it?"

Antonelli permitted himself a faint smile. "I am accustomed to a higher standard of dancing," he admitted.

Thatcher could imagine the encounter. Miss Maas and Antonelli were both used to calling the tune. She probably expected disproportionate gratitude for any favors she bestowed. He moved in a world where he could take his pick of nameless pretty girls to squire to sumptuous house parties.

Antonelli, in fact, had the air of a loner amidst all these exuberant young people.

"I gather that Miss Maas was too busy to see the ice skating this evening," Thatcher said. "Did you?"

"Of course. What else was there to do?"

"I thought the performances by Suzanne Deladier and the Russian girl were quite exceptional."

"They were very fine indeed," Antonelli agreed amiably.

Thatcher himself had stonewalled too often not to recognize the technique. Carlo Antonelli had no intention of discussing his desires, his habits or his views. Without abating his good manners, he would return perfunctory agreement to every remark until his inquisitor was stupefied by boredom. Thatcher retreated into more impersonal areas.

"I see that almost everyone is here tonight, and that is understandable with no outdoor events tomorrow. But what about those who are competing? Miss Deladier and Miss Darskaya, for instance, are going to meet in a dramatic duel tomorrow. Do they relax here after today's bout or do they go to bed early for tomorrow's?"

Antonelli seemed to welcome the change in approach. "It's a matter of individual temperament. Suzanne Deladier, I believe, has not joined us. The Russian girl I am almost sure I recognized earlier." Then he uttered an exclamation. "But look who is here, Mr. Thatcher."

Swiveling in his chair, Thatcher saw Tilly Lowengard standing on the threshold of the room. Her escort was Dick Noyes, but they were not alone. Surrounding Tilly was a whole platoon of stern-faced young men. Thatcher recognized Gunther Euler towering above the rest.

Tilly paused in the doorway, blocking traffic and deliberately inviting attention. Conversation at one table after another died away until even the dancers, sensing something unusual, faltered and came to rest.

Then, from far back in the disco a single yell rang out.

"Attagirl, Tilly!"

Instantly a clear British voice echoed, "Cheers, Tilly!"

And suddenly the whole room was stamping and applauding.

Tilly, her jaw outthrust and her level gaze fixed, was taken aback. She had nerved herself to outface hostility and the wave of approval broke through her defenses. Blushing rosily, she clasped her hands to her lips and looked around in confusion until her companions took over. They secured a table by simply waving away its occupants, seated Tilly as if they were enthroning her, then plunked themselves down in a protective circle. Their outriders began to drift away, one of them coming to rest by Thatcher and Antonelli.

"These Swiss know how to do things," Gunther

Euler remarked enthusiastically. "It's time we all had a chance to show how we feel about the IOC."

Even as he was moving his chair over to make room, Antonelli shook his head. "I think you're wrong, Euler. People are just showing how they feel about Tilly Lowengard."

"Then you haven't heard what the IOC said to the Swiss team manager. Christ, you've been around the Olympics long enough to know they think they can treat us like dirt. They make up silly rules, throw us out on a whim and think nobody should even ask questions."

The hotter Euler became, the cooler Antonelli grew. "Well, they seem to be able to get away with it."

"That's what makes a demonstration like this so important. For once we've all rallied behind an IOC scapegoat."

Antonelli shrugged. "So you've rallied. What good will it do? The IOC is right across the hall at the buffet. Do you think they're going to change their minds because they can hear applause for Tilly? She'll be on her way as soon as they open a road."

But Euler was showing a stubborn dedication to someone else's cause that Thatcher would never have anticipated. "They've got to listen if we all complain about their arbitrary regulations."

"No they don't." There was a glint in Antonelli's eye as he continued. "But I'll tell you something that might help Tilly. After all, they can't hold the Games without us. We could start a boycott. You could say you won't compete in the jumping."

Euler flinched as if he had been stung. "When I've practically got the gold medal in my hand? I'd have to be crazy."

"That's what I thought."

"It's all right for you. You just fool around bobsledding to pass the time. But I'm serious about jumping," Euler continued to justify himself.

Antonelli, however, had lost interest. "I didn't think it would be a popular suggestion," he murmured.

Euler looked in two minds about continuing the discussion. Then, clamping his mouth shut, he levered himself to his feet. "I think I'll find myself a partner," he said stiffly. "This is supposed to be a disco."

After he had gone, Antonelli was mildly apologetic. "I don't know why Euler gets to me," he confessed. "But Tilly Lowengard has enough trouble without his trying to turn her into his own personal bandwagon."

"You don't think he's sincere in his attack on the IOC's high-handedness?" Thatcher asked.

"Let's say I don't believe it's the drugging regulation he's worried about," Antonelli said shortly, then changed the subject. "I think I'll drop by Tilly's table and say an encouraging word. Do you want to come or does your official capacity make it embarrassing to acknowledge an IOC mistake?"

"I'm not official at all," said Thatcher, sinking his appearances as Withers' deputy, "and I can't say that I care for the IOC's methods. But what makes you assume an error? I thought the urine sample technique was foolproof."

The mask of long-suffering that clouded the Italian's face was familiar to Thatcher. It signaled the yawning of a gigantic generation gap. For most social purposes, Antonelli would qualify as part of the herd of indistinguishable adults. But on the subject of drugs, he would inevitably regard anyone Thatcher's age as impossibly ignorant.

"It is really quite simple," he said with exaggerated patience. "There are uppers and there are downers.

Plenty of contestants will hype themselves with an upper if they think they can get away with it. Nobody in their right mind would take a downer just before competition. The test they ran at the Medical Center merely proved there was an alien substance. But you saw Tilly ski, you were standing right next to me. Every athlete there, as soon as he got over the shock, realized she had been heavily sedated. In other words, somebody slipped her a Mickey."

No wonder the Swiss delegation was up in arms!

"And she had a good chance of winning," Thatcher mused, following his own line of thought.

"An excellent chance."

Under these circumstances, Thatcher decided to follow his inclination and join Antonelli's mission. They found Tilly a good deal more realistic about displays of support than Euler had been.

"Oh, it's kind of everybody and I appreciate it. But it isn't what I want," she exclaimed, running a hand frantically through her short crop. "I want the IOC to listen to me and they won't!"

"You wouldn't believe the way they're acting," Dick Noyes burst forth. It was plain to Thatcher that this was his first encounter with bull-headed officialdom. "They refused to meet formally with the team reps and then, when Egon and Bernard tried to talk to Melville at the skating tonight, he threatened to have them thrown out of the box."

There was a sullen mutter of assent from the blond giants at the table.

"It's more than the IOC, much more." Tilly spread her brown workmanlike hands in a gesture of despair. "Everything's been crazy for days. First they claim I've been passing counterfeit. Then they say I've been stuffing myself with drugs in order to make sure I'll lose.

The next thing I know, they'll be accusing me of murdering Yves Bisson and have some fantastic evidence to prove it."

"Tilly!" Dick Noyes was aghast.

She looked at him steadily. "Well, we have to face it, Dick. That's the biggest crime around that somebody has to be saddled with, and I seem to be the favorite target for that sort of thing." She caught herself on a half-choking breath. "Oh, I know I sound paranoid. But I don't know what's going on! If I did, I'd feel better even if there were nothing I could do."

Dick had grasped her hand and was half-crooning. "Tilly, Tilly, you're letting it get to you. We'll figure something out, you'll see. We'll get the IOC to listen to reason."

"Fat chance," rumbled one of the giants.

Dick cast him a look of dislike and abruptly shoved his chair back. "This isn't getting us anywhere, Tilly. C'mon, let's dance."

Their departure loosened tongues.

"Noyes is a fool if he is still thinking in terms of appeals to reason," remarked the rumbler.

He was contradicted instantly. "Nonsense, Bernard. Tilly is entitled to a full hearing and this is no time to give up. It was probably a mistake trying to talk to Melville in his box. Perhaps we should prepare a brief outlining Tilly's rights."

"Egon, when will you abandon stereotyped thinking?" Bernard shook his head sorrowfully. "You have not considered the power structure we are dealing with."

"And you have, I suppose?"

"Certainly." Bernard was very calm. "The IOC has said there is no benefit to be derived from a discussion with us. Remembering that they are quite dense, we must simply create a situation in which the benefits are self-apparent."

Egon sounded hopeful. "You've thought of something?"

"Yes." Bernard's gaze rested momentarily on Thatcher and Antonelli. "I'll tell you about it later."

Thatcher could take a hint as well as the next man. But, as he left the table, he realized that his first impression of the Swiss had been misleading. He had allowed himself to be distracted by their massive forms and lithe vigor. Instead he should have noticed that Bernard's eyes were alarmingly intelligent.

After the Swiss, John Thatcher would have appreciated a respite. But it was not to be.

"John!"

Brad Withers was excusing himself to a companion before padding over to his vice-president. The companion was very young, very blond, and very pretty. It was only to be expected. Years ago Thatcher had noticed that a day starting with a hectoring phone call from Caroline Withers was likely to end with Brad being ponderously gallant to some sweet young thing.

"Do you know who that is?" Brad asked in triumph.

Thatcher frowned. There was indeed something familiar about the tilt of that head, the carriage of those shoulders. But Brad was too impatient for the slow process of recollection.

"That's Vera Darskaya, the Russian ice skater," he said proudly. "You remember, she was tied with the French girl."

"Of course I do."

"Now I don't like to see you standing here, out of things, John. You come back and join us."

It would be impossible to convince Withers that anyone standing alone, however briefly, did not yearn for integration into the nearest group.

"Perhaps a little later," Thatcher temporized.

Withers leaned forward and lowered his voice to an alcoholic hush. "Now this is strictly confidential, John, but Vera Andreevna has something on her mind."

"I'm sure she has," said Thatcher at random.

"And we'd both appreciate your advice."

But before Thatcher was forced to commit himself, he saw rescue at hand. In the doorway stood Captain Phil Ormsby.

And just as Thatcher saw him, he spotted Thatcher. He raised a hand in a gesture of invitation—or was it command?

"If you'll excuse me for a minute," said Thatcher. "I think the police want me."

"But, John . . ."

Bradford Withers' voice followed him for all of three feet.

13 EMERGENCY VEHICLES

ORMSBY wasted no time. "You remember how we were wondering yesterday what Vaux and the Maas woman could be up to?"

"Certainly. You accused me of being biased in favor of paper crime."

Ormsby was in high spirits. "Well, I think we're going to settle it for good tonight. I thought you might like to come along."

"Come where?" asked Thatcher. "The only road in the area that's open is the one downtown."

"Leave that part to me. Just be at the front door in five minutes."

Thatcher was still fastening his parka when Ormsby's cavalcade pulled up. It consisted of two military-looking vehicles equipped with plows, four-wheel drives and tire chains. The police inside all looked ready to climb Mount Everest.

"Are you sure anything will happen tonight?" Thatcher asked mildly after he had bundled himself into the seat next to Ormsby. "It seems an odd time for a criminal to move around inconspicuously."

"These are odd criminals," rejoined the police captain. He was still hugging a secret joke to himself. "But we know they're going into action tonight. One of my men spotted Katarina Maas sneaking out of Olympic Village, and François Vaux wasn't far behind her. Incidentally, I was right about those two not being paper shufflers. When they see something they want to steal, they simply take it."

There was no doubt that they had moved from speculation to fact. Thatcher was impressed.

"How have you managed to find out so much since yesterday? Particularly in view of the conditions. The Village must have been in chaos yesterday night and this morning."

"I started at the other end, that's how," said Ormsby in tones of self-congratulation. "I went to the big outfit that's supplying the Village, the one I told you about, and asked them who'd be in the best position to fence stolen commissary supplies. They gave me three names in the area and it turned out to be the second one. I struck it real lucky, thanks to Vaux's itchy fingers and the high price of French cheese. There were ten sides of beef that the guy didn't have invoices for, but I would have had a hard time proving origin. Thank God there was this one case of Brie that still had the customs seal on it. After that, we didn't have any more trouble. He told me all about tonight's little arrangement."

As the rendezvous must have been scheduled before the arrival of the blizzard, Thatcher was still doubtful.

"I hope that Vaux is as indifferent to the weather as you are," he said tactfully.

"Oh, this weather is all to the good from his point of

view." Ormsby's confidence was unimpaired. "Incidentally, you realize that this whole setup is irregular."

"Considering how you dragooned me into this commando raid, it's a little late to worry about my presence, isn't it?"

Ormsby hastened to explain. "I don't mean you, I mean me. Theoretically this is a little side issue that I should leave to the local boys. But I'm hoping that once we can stick Vaux and Maas with a charge, they'll loosen up with anything they know about Yves Bisson and his operation."

"Now, that I'll go along with."

They were the last words Thatcher was capable of speaking for some time. The pavement had just ended. Their vehicle, however, plunged straight ahead. The difference in terrain was immediately apparent. The cover varied from a foot of powder snow, to deep drifts, to sudden bare icy patches. Nothing stopped Captain Ormsby's convoy. The semi-tanks crunched along, skidding, recovering, climbing, thudding into drops. Thatcher grabbed a protruding metal strut and concentrated on keeping his head from bashing into the roof.

"How much farther?" he managed to gasp after three miles of pounding.

"We're almost there. It's that four corners where Vaux and Maas were hanging around the day before Bisson was shot."

When they arrived, the motel was not quite invisible, its outdoor lighting creating a pearly glow in the snowfall.

"Everybody's gone to bed," Ormsby grunted as he registered the darkened facade. "Probably bored to death."

Thatcher wondered briefly if this was where the unfortunate French were entombed. But no, this one at least had a coffee shop, he recalled. Some of them didn't even have that.

Ormsby was clambering stiffly down. "All right, boys," he directed. "I want these trucks out of sight in the bays of that garage. Then we're going to have a half-hour wait, so we'll hope that there's some heat in the office."

As Thatcher himself dismounted, he considered the captain's strategy. Clearly it was intended to provide a superficially unoccupied vista so that the malefactors would walk into the trap. The vehicles would be out of sight. The police would be lurking in a darkened office. But . . . As one of the trucks reversed into the gas station, its powerful headlights lit up the road by which they had come.

"Do you think half an hour is enough to cover our tracks, Captain?" he asked doubtfully. "I know it's snowing steadily, but we seem to have churned up quite a wake."

Ormsby shrugged. "I think it'll do the job. Besides, they won't be coming from that direction."

Thatcher's eyebrows climbed to his hairline. Instinctively, he swung around to examine the smooth white ribbon that signaled the further progression of the road up the hill that stood between them and Saranac. Why in the world should Vaux and Maas be coming from that direction? Surely the whole point of their operation was to move goods away from Lake Placid, not toward it.

What began as a lack of faith in the police plan soon hardened into complete mistrust under the impact of physical discomfort. There was, in fact, a small inadequate electric heater. There were also giant gaps around the ill-fitting windows and door that admitted brisk gusts of wind. To add to the general joy Captain Ormsby, at the twenty-minute mark, forbade all foot stamping and hand clapping. At the thirty-minute mark, as far as Thatcher was concerned, his circulation ceased. At the forty-five-minute mark, Ormsby raised a finger, cocked his head and smiled.

"Listen."

In a second Thatcher heard it too. It was a high-pitched, laboring whine.

"But that's not a car," he protested. "And it's not even coming from the road."

Indeed it sounded to him like some maniac with a chain saw in the woods far behind the gas station.

"Snowmobiles," Ormsby explained tersely. "There's an old logging track that comes out here."

As Thatcher absorbed this new factor, he remembered the daredevils he had seen whizzing around the outskirts of Lake Placid. "Surely they go faster than that."

"Not when they're pulling a string of loaded sledges." Ormsby was relaxing now that he was assured of a fruitful night's work. "Okay, boys. Open the door and get ready to move. They should be pulling up in a few minutes."

A string of loaded sledges! Well, why not? Thatcher had to admit that it was logical. In the great rum-running days, there were portions of the English coast littered with trains of loaded mules. Allowing for different weather conditions and different technology, this was much the same thing. Instead of a single smuggler carrying a hooded lantern, there would soon be a headlight.

No sooner had the thought crossed his mind than he could distinguish an elfin halo dancing in and out of trees. Then the flickering resolved itself into two dis-

140

tinct sources. The lead light clarified, its accompanying buzzsaw grew louder, and then a dark shape glided into the clearing.

The young troopers at the door were too precipitate. Waiting only for the engine to die, they surged forward announcing they were police. The second snowmobile, with a clear view of the proceedings, still had plenty of room to maneuver and its driver reacted with lightning reflexes. Gunning the motor savagely, he swung around the tangle by the shed and then swept into a wide arc at full throttle. Above the snarling roar came the click of a safety release and, like ice skaters playing snap the whip, six loaded sledges tumbled free. The sliding semicircle effectively cut off the police, their trucks and, incidentally, the first snowmobile.

"François, you pig!" screamed Katarina Maas.

"My God, he's going to get away with it," groaned Captain Ormsby, watching helplessly as the fleeing driver charged the hill to Saranac.

The words were barely out of his mouth when a powerful beacon of light appeared over the crest, and a giant roar heralded the advance of a third machine, on collison course with the fugitive.

"Jesus Christ, who's that?"

The police might be at a loss, but François Vaux never doubted that this was another element in the ambush. Snapping into a precipitous U-turn, he made a desperate bid for the road to Lake Placid, only to meet his nemesis in the outermost sledge. His machine smashed into the obstacle and heeled over, while Vaux himself was neatly pitched into the waiting arms of a trooper.

Meanwhile the snowmobile from Saranac that had arrived so opportunely coasted decorously down the hill, ran into the yard and halted. Two riders dismounted and approached. Silhouetted from behind by their own headlight, they might have been two visitors from outer space in their snowmobile suits and helmets and boots. But from one distorted hulk came a very familiar voice.

"We regret there has been an accident and hope there has been no personal injury. We stand ready to provide any assistance we can."

"I don't think that will be necessary," Ormsby began.

But the voice swept on. "However, I must protest the gross negligence with which this driver was operating his vehicle. In view of the hazardous road conditions—"

"Everett!"

It took quite some time to dissuade Everett Gabler from formulating his defense against a possible insurance claim.

"This is a police trap, Everett, that you've walked into. But how in the world did you get here? None of the roads or the airports are open."

This was meat and drink to Gabler.

"I have often had occasion to remind our junior staff that closing normal transport routes does not render any locale inaccessible. It simply means that more thought is required in attaining one's goal."

"Yes, Everett, I've heard you on the subject."

What's more, Gabler's practice was as good as his preaching. Thatcher, for one, never doubted that if Everett had had an appointment in San Francisco on that historic day in 1906, he would have been there on the dot. As the San Andreas Fault heaved and water mains blew up and the city burned to the ground, he would have watched the clock tick past the hour, fulminating steadily about the irresponsibility of his

absent host. Difficulties, after all, are made to be overcome.

"And did you overcome them this time?"

According to Everett, it had been simplicity itself. A
short air hop to Albany, followed by dog hops on little-
known feeder railroads, had brought him to Saranac.

"And there, I was fortunately able to persuade Mr.
Sturgess to carry me on his machine."

Introductions were hastily made. Mr. Sturgess, naturally, turned out to be a thoroughly reliable, middle-
aged stalwart who saw nothing strange in Everett's
proceedings.

Ormsby was amused at the entire incident. "Well,
you turned up in the nick of time. And I'm glad to see
that part of your bank knows about snowmobiles. You
people should get your act together."

Unfortunately he then went on to explain the nature
of their night's activity. Gabler was sorry to see Thatcher wasting his time this way.

"Of course I understand this is a legitimate concern
of the police," he said graciously to Ormsby. "Indeed,
I expected to find the authorities preoccupied with the
murder of that ski jumper. We all recognize the superior claims of a threat to human life." He paused to
bend a steely gaze on his delinquent chief. "But, John,
we should certainly not forget that the Sloan has suffered very substantial losses through a scheme that
could easily be repeated at any moment."

Thatcher thought of all the precautions now exer-
cised by Roger Hathaway.

"Not easily," he demurred.

"And it is for that very reason that I decided not to
defer a consultation with you until more clement
weather."

Ormsby, who believed in leaving family fights to the

family, intervened. "I'm hoping that tonight's catch may shed some light on your problem. But it's high time I got on with it. Why don't we load up and get back to town? There'll be room for you, too, Mr. Gabler."

Cleaning-up operations were accomplished with dispatch. Two troopers were left to guard the evidence, which included more sides of beef than Thatcher had ever seen outside of a warehouse. The prisoners went in one truck, and the senior members of the party climbed into the other.

"I'll let you know if Vaux and Maas come up with anything," Ormsby promised en route.

"Are you hopeful?"

"You never can tell. Maas and Vaux are going to take this differently. It sticks out all over them. The woman has never been caught before. Right now, she's spitting mad and trying to blame somebody else for her troubles. She'll probably clam up and yell for a lawyer. But Vaux's been there before and he's always managed to wriggle clear. He's already thinking of ways to make a deal. That should make him pretty cooperative."

"Unless," Thatcher pointed out, "what he has to tell would get him into even worse trouble."

"Yes, there's always that," Ormsby agreed as they pulled up to the motel. "But we'll know by tomorrow."

Gabler had been champing at the bit during this exchange. Nonetheless he omitted not one detail from his meticulous leavetaking. He even stood on the sidewalk to watch the trucks pull off. Then he took a mighty breath.

"And now, John," he said severely, "perhaps we could turn our attention to these Eurochecks."

14 ZERO VISIBILITY

EVERETT Gabler's hopes for a rewarding work session at two o'clock in the morning were dashed the moment they entered the Sloan's motel suite. The bank's president was already there, wrapped in a benign alcoholic haze and struggling ineffectually with his elaborate ski boots.

Brad Withers' instincts were patriarchal. He liked nothing better than to gather members of the great Sloan family under his wing and offer them the best he had.

"Everett! Isn't this wonderful!" he cried with innocent enthusiasm. "You're in time to see the women's figure skating tomorrow."

Fortunately Brad never noticed anybody else's reactions.

"I will certainly bear that in mind," Gabler promised in tones of loathing. "But it's already quite late and, if we are to do anything tomorrow, I suggest we all retire."

Thus it was not until the following morning that

145

Thatcher and Gabler were able to huddle with Roger Hathaway at the Sloan branch, for the kind of discussion so dear to Everett's heart.

"Now," he purred, spreading his notes on the table, "I think you'll agree with me that the situation is most interesting."

"That's not the way I'd describe it," said Hathaway gruffly. "Somebody's ripped me off for half a million."

Gabler always liked to see the bank's young officers identifying with the Sloan. He nodded approvingly as he continued.

"That aspect is deplorable, it goes without saying. But the matter does not end there. It is our clear duty to utilize our special expertise in order to recover the loss."

Hathaway blinked. "But that's a job for the police."

Normally this would have provoked a broadside about the relative competence of state authorities and the Sloan. But Gabler, who had been mellowing by the minute since separation from Withers, was unusually forbearing.

"The police, no doubt, are doing their best. I was favorably impressed by Captain Ormsby last night. But they will surely welcome any assistance we can give them." Gabler cleared his throat to signal the end of the preliminaries. "Now the first thing I did was communicate with Eurocheck headquarters overseas. Since they are a comparatively new organization, they have no experience with intensive investigations. I regret to say we cannot expect any reinforcements from them— even if they could get here."

Thatcher was not deceived. Every institution that issues what amounts to cash has to protect the validity of that currency. The United States Government maintains a Secret Service; American Express employs an army of security personnel. If Eurocheck had been as old or as large as either, there would have been swarms of their agents in Lake Placid, dropped by parachute if necessary. Everett was pleased as punch to be spared this competition.

"They have, however, been uniformly helpful in supplying details," Gabler swept on. "I don't have to tell you that the dislocations in transport have stranded many European tour groups heading for the Olympic Games. They are almost all in New York or Montreal."

Thatcher's interest quickened. "Where they have been cashing checks steadily for over twenty-four hours."

"And the forgeries have been isolated to one charter. Everybody else has bona fide Eurochecks."

"Let me guess, Everett," Thatcher said. "That one group is a bunch of Frenchmen from Grenoble."

Gabler was a stickler for detail. "Not from Grenoble, no. But in spirit, you're right. The tour was organized through Yves Bisson's travel agency for a skating club that wanted to see Suzanne Deladier. They've been in Montreal now for almost two days."

"But that doesn't do any good," Roger Hathaway protested. "We already knew that Bisson was using his agency to funnel the phonies."

Both Thatcher and Gabler looked at him reproachfully. He was losing sight of essentials.

"You've got hold of the wrong end of the stick, Hathaway," Thatcher explained. "Forget Bisson. This tells us that nobody else in Europe was selling counterfeits. For instance, I was inclined to suspect Katarina Maas because of her contacts with travel arrangements in Europe. It now turns out that no use was made of charter groups originating overseas—with the single exception of Yves Bisson's agency. We're not dealing with a widespread foreign network. We're dealing with a small gang right here in Lake Placid."

Hathaway was still doubtful. "If you say so."

"I know so," Thatcher replied resoundingly. "You might bring Everett up to date on your own experiences at the bank since the blizzard."

Here, at last, was a subject on which Roger Hathaway was the expert. "It was like I expected. We did a land office business at the Olympic Village branch. We had a total of twelve forgeries show up at the counter."

"And you asked where those checks were physically located in the flaps?"

"They were all at the back of the flaps," Hathaway agreed.

Gabler wasted no time in following up. "What about the spectators? I'll wager that there were no forgeries there."

"No, there weren't. But I don't know how much that means. We had virtually no business in the other branches. Most of the tourists couldn't get outside."

"Bah!" Gabler swept away this trifling caveat. "It's as clear as a bell."

Thatcher was not feeling quite so triumphant. Academic clarity was desirable, but not as desirable as half a million in hand. "It's clear now, Everett," he said thoughtfully. "But only because we've been lucky."

"Lucky!" Hathaway snorted.

"Lucky in that the gang's timing has been thrown off, right from the start. First there was Bisson's faux pas, when he paid for the snowmobile rental. That forced them to stage their coup prematurely. Then this blizzard has frozen everyboby in place for forty-eight extra hours. Consider what would have happened if the timetable had gone according to schedule. There would have been a massive hit on the Sloan the last day of the Games. Then, with spectators and athletes dispersing, counterfeits would have surfaced in New York and Washington and Montreal, and even back in Europe, for at least a week. The whole issue would have been confused."

Without admitting that he would have been misled, Everett Gabler sidestepped the question.

"On the whole I am tempted to think that Bisson's activities were mere window dressing."

"More like salting a gold mine," Thatcher corrected. "His major contribution was made in Grenoble with those two charter groups. After that, he simply lurked around Olympic Village planting as many forgeries as possible. It was the others in Lake Placid who did the important work, passing the half-million."

Roger Hathaway had weighed every word. "I see the point you're making about Bisson. But how can you be so sure the gang is in Lake Placid? Maybe they just came in for the day."

"No, look at the speed with which they acted when their schedule was blown to smithereens. You've forgotten the difficulty of getting into Lake Placid. Cars are forbidden and you have to show tickets for the Games to bus in. Needless to say, those tickets were all disposed of months ago. Even so, the moment they learned of Bisson's mistake, they moved up their plans by several days."

Gabler coughed severely. "Not to mention the fact that they murdered Bisson."

"Precisely. They must have been here all along. And anybody in Lake Placid on a permanent basis right now has to be part of the Olympic family. They are not simply day trippers with a ticket for the biathlon."

"You've got to be right," Hathaway said slowly.

"Just the murder alone should have told me. Captain Ormsby was awfully interested in the people who were with Bisson when he rented that snowmobile."

Gabler reviewed what he knew. "What is the significance of the group that accompanied Bisson? Why them in particular?"

John Thatcher explained with a description of Yves Bisson's last outing. "So you see," he concluded, "the police are going on the assumption that Bisson's confederates actually saw his error."

Gabler rubbed his hands together zestfully. "Now we're beginning to narrow things down. This is a relatively small number of people, and all strategically located. And we already know there are two criminals included among them."

"Well, Everett, you're the one who has supplied most of our information about five of the seven," Thatcher reminded him. "And it hasn't helped that much."

"Surely more personal investigation is possible."

Hathaway was almost shamefaced. "As a matter of fact, I thought about that. So I've been spending most of my evenings at the disco in the Village. I didn't want to say anything about it unless I came up with something."

His seniors sympathized. It would be a real feather in Roger Hathaway's cap if he could make a substantial contribution to solving the case.

"And have you come to any conclusions about the kind of people they are?" Thatcher asked.

"It's not as easy as you think to get on friendly terms with them. For one thing, I'm too old."

To Everett, of course, Hathaway was a mere stripling. "What do you mean by that?" he demanded. "I realize that some of them are barely out of their teens. But this man, Antonelli, is as old as you are."

It was Roger Hathaway's turn to explain the facts of life. "It's the girls I dance with, Mr. Gabler."

"Yes, yes," said Thatcher hastily. "With what luck?"

Hathaway shook his head. "Not much. The Maas girl spent half an hour finding out if I was rich. When she found out I wasn't, she gave me the brush. Tilly Lowengard just seems to like to dance. And I never even got to the floor with Suzanne Deladier. So mostly I've just been listening to the chatter. Antonelli is pretty well-off. He bobsleds because he likes it. Gunther Euler is hoping to make it into the big time with an Olympic medal. And Dick Noyes acts like a college kid who happens to be a good skier. I don't think I'm cut out for this kind of detective work."

It did not sound like a fruitful haul and Gabler had no hesitation in saying so. "Even the Maas woman does not look hopeful. I find it difficult to believe that she would spend her nights stealing a thousand dollars' worth of beef, if she were involved in a half-million-dollar crime."

There was a discouraged silence until Thatcher stirred. He had a statement he felt had to be made.

"There is one further item. We have explored the consequences to the criminals of their shattered timetable. They were forced into murder and increased risk of detection. Under the circumstances, wouldn't you think they would want to leave Lake Placid as quickly as possible?"

Gabler was delighted to spot the flaw in his colleague's reasoning. "They may wish to, but they cannot. Not without a flight that is tantamount to a confession of guilt. We have already proved that they are here in some official capacity."

Thatcher was almost sad. "But there is one person who would already be gone, if it were not for the blizzard. Has it occurred to you that Tilly Lowengard may have arranged to be thrown out? If by any chance she wants to flee a possible murder charge, that would be a remarkably clever way to do it. Not to leave voluntarily, but to be expelled."

Gabler accepted the suggestion placidly, but he had not danced with Tilly.

"You can't be serious," exploded Hathaway. "That girl a major criminal! I don't believe it."

Thatcher was not immune to these sentiments himself. But a lifetime of banking had brought to his attention charming young con men with absolutely no scruples and pretty young tellers with itchy fingers. He had even dealt with sweet white-haired ladies whose embezzlements were enriching their church's missionary fund. It took more than a nut-brown complexion to prove innocence.

"I'm afraid we have to consider it," he said.

At Police Headquarters there was less contention. François Vaux and Captain Ormsby might have been two tired co-workers. As Ormsby had predicted, Katarina Maas had already snarled her way to a lawyer and bail. But Vaux was doggedly concentrating on a reduction in charge.

"A first offense?" he repeated suggestively. "I'm simply a poor man tempted by all that wealth around me. And my career has been ended. That is a big punishment by itself. Surely we can be reasonable about this."

Ormsby had already come to the same conclusion as Everett Gabler. People pulling off a big caper do not fill their spare time lugging sides of beef around the countryside.

"I don't say that isn't possible. But you'd have to make it worth my while." He shoved aside the debris of sandwiches and coffee with which the two had been regaling themselves. "You know damn well I'm not interested in your two-bit larceny. I'm interested in Yves Bisson."

"You have only to ask," Vaux said fervently.

"How well did you know him?"

"Quite well. The ski-jumping world is smaller than the alpine skiing world, you know. And it is dominated by the Scandinavians and the East Germans. There are relatively few Frenchmen. I met Yves when he first emerged in national competition about five years ago. But we were not sufficiently intimate for him to confide his criminal plans to me."

Ormsby guffawed. The Vauxs of this world were all too familiar to him. "I'll bet he didn't. If he had, you'd have wanted a cut."

"Captain, Captain." Vaux spread his hands placatingly. "I don't have to tell you that I'm not a big international mastermind. It is true that I pick up what I can—a little here, a little there. I blame it all on this credit economy. A man's debts are always larger than his income. So I do what is necessary to bridge the gap."

Ormsby was inclined to agree. Vaux's record spoke for itself. Small temptations and small crimes were his style. He was not looking for trouble. It would never occur to him to initiate a major theft, and the thought of murder would terrify him.

"All right, so Bisson didn't confide his plans. But does the fact that he had some surprise the hell out of you?"

Vaux cocked his head and studied the matter. "No, I cannot say that it does. Ski competition takes you into the world of the rich. Yves came from a limited background and, suddenly, he was seeing what it was like in St. Moritz and Zermatt. At the beginning he was like all the youngsters. He was content to have the entree to that world, to be something of a celebrity, to concentrate on winning. But a man cannot ski all year. He has to come back to reality for months at a time. And Yves didn't want to. He wanted money and he began to look for it."

"How?"

"Oh, nothing to concern you." Vaux shrugged. "He wanted to know how much he could get for equipment endorsements if he took a gold medal. He complained at the greater commercial opportunities for downhill skiers. He became an expert at being funded under the table. But it was never enough."

"So you think he began to think along different lines."

Vaux shook his head. "I doubt if he had the imagination to do that. But he would have been open to suggestion, almost any suggestion. He had decided that was the way the world worked."

Ormsby sighed and looked not too hopefully at his abandoned coffee cup. There was not even one sip left. The psychology of a money-hungry athlete was interesting, but not particularly helpful.

"Let's forget about his character for a minute," he suggested. "What about Bisson while he was here at Lake Placid. Was he preoccupied? Was his jumping all right?"

"He was jumping very well. I had told him again and again that his takeoffs were the problem in the

154

World Cup. And he was hitting them just right. The seventy-meter jump had been his specialty until this year, but now he was coming strongly in the ninety-meter. Why, in one of his practice jumps he did a hundred and seventeen meters, and he would not have lost on style points. He was—"

Ormsby held up a hand. He had forgotten that Vaux, in addition to being a small-time thief, was a technical expert.

"Okay, so whatever he was into, it wasn't affecting his spirits or his work. Now about this snowmobile outing."

"He seemed as always to me." Vaux paused to grimace ruefully. "It was I who was upset. You understand we were not pleased, Katarina and I, to find them all there. We did not want it generally known that we were familiars at that snowmobile station. And we were right!"

"Never mind about that now. So Bisson was normal."

"More exuberant than usual. But that was natural. He was very close to that gold medal and all those endorsements. It was Euler who was forcing gaiety."

Ormsby pounced instantly. "Euler wasn't happy, you say. Was that before or after Bisson paid with a Euro-check?"

Vaux was trying to be cooperative. He wrinkled his brow in a tortured effort at recollection. Finally he groaned. "I cannot be absolutely certain. I think I noticed it just as they were leaving. But I accepted that, you understand. Euler was seeing a gold slip from his grasp and trying not to show it. Anyway, that is the interpretation I put on it."

And it was an interpretation that would not be questioned, except for the fact that another explanation loomed more ominously.

Vaux was genuinely sorry not to have pinned it down for the captain. "I regret I cannot be more specific. But at the time I was simply wishing them all at perdition. I was not really myself until that evening." He cast around for something to mollify the police. "But I can tell you one more thing I noticed."

"Oh yeah?" growled Ormsby. "What's that? You weren't even on the bus when Bisson realized he'd made a blooper."

"But I have heard much talk about that trip and how discomposed Yves became. Of that I know nothing. But by evening he had resolved his problem."

Ormsby looked up. By that evening Yves Bisson should have realized the implications of his mistake, he should have been anticipating a call by the police. God knows, his confederates had been quick enough to figure that one out.

"How's that? How could he have resolved his problem?"

Vaux was earnest. "I do not know. But I knew Yves, and I spoke with him at some length about the next day's practice. I can assure you of this. By that evening, he did not have a care in the world!"

The same could not be said for the Sloan contingent. Apart from their own lack of progress, the first reports from the band of specialists at the Andiron Inn were not calculated to induce foolish optimism.

"They've started to work down the list of commercial depositors," Thatcher relayed. "Most motel owners and restaurateurs don't even remember what was on their deposit slips."

"For God's sake!" Hathaway exclaimed. "How have

they managed to tackle my list? Half those places are still inaccessible."

Thatcher shook his head reprovingly. "Don't be misled by the Olympic atmosphere, Hathaway. I know that yesterday began with your opening the branches on skis, and it ended with Everett's breaking through to Lake Placid on a snowmobile, but Milliken's bunch seems to manage quite well with standard operating procedures. At any rate, I told him we'd stop by to look at their haul."

As they filed through the lobby, Thatcher let his companions go ahead and halted by the switchboard. Meticulously informing the girl of their destination, he learned the reason for her harassed expression.

"Oh, Mr. Thatcher," she said, duly making a note, "you wouldn't know where Mr. Withers is, would you? I have the IOC on the line and they can't locate him."

By rights, Brad should have been laid up with the granddaddy of all hangovers. But his powers of recuperation had caused trouble more than once in the past.

"Tell them to try the skating arena," Thatcher advised.

On the sidewalk he found Gabler and Hathaway watching a burst of activity across the street. Men were leaping into cars and gunning down the road, a crew was manhandling long ladders over a snowbank and into the back of a truck, dignitaries from Town Hall were emerging onto the freshly shoveled steps and delivering last-minute instructions.

"Something's up," Hathaway observed.

"I daresay there's a good deal of activity involved in reopening this community," Gabler rejoined. "But whatever is going on, we can safely assume it has nothing to do with our counterfeit Eurochecks."

He was out by a country mile.

15 UPPER-LEVEL DISTURBANCE

ALL those men and trucks were heading for Whiteface Mountain, where the drama being played out was of more importance to the Sloan Guaranty Trust than any of the principal characters imagined. Ironically, in view of the events scheduled for that location, attention was centered on a stationary object. The aerial tramway had been halted and two cable cars, neatly balancing each other, swayed in the breeze far from their supporting pylons. The down car was empty.

Inside the other gondola, forcibly marooned, Anthony Melville and several companions dangled high above the precipitous slope.

Newcomers to the scene, when they heard that the Swiss team had hijacked the tramway, could scarcely believe their ears. How, they demanded, could such a thing have happened?

The explanation was simple enough. Melville, relaxing in the genial atmosphere of the disco the previous evening, had been too loose-tongued. As soon as he received word from the Olympic maintenance people, he said, he intended to ascend Whiteface and personally inspect the progress of trail grooming.

It therefore seemed only natural to him when his lunch ended with a telephone call purporting to come from a grounds supervisor. He had immediately collected his assistants and trundled out to the base station. There, all unsuspecting, the party had entered the cable car waiting for them. Melville had never noticed that the attendants were a trifle more ceremonious than usual, a trifle less chatty.

He had noticed plenty, however, when the tramway came to a stop and the radio in the corner began barking.

"Mr. Melville, this is Bernard Heise of the Swiss team speaking. We have seized control of the funicular system in order to discuss the case of Mathilde Lowengard."

The accents were familiar. Dimly Melville remembered that voice from a troublesome encounter in his box at the skating arena.

"Young man," he said promptly, "I have nothing to say to you."

This pronouncement, splendidly boomed, was wasted. An aide slithered across the pitching floor to deliver a short lecture on the use of the R/T radio.

"You have to punch this button to talk, Mr. Melville, and then you say it into the microphone. When you're done, you hit this button to hear the answer."

Melville, never at his best with machinery, muffed the first attempt. It was now too late to recapture his initial fervor.

"I have nothing to say to you, young man," he repeated dully.

"That is entirely satisfactory," replied Bernard. "It is what I have to say that is important."

Bernard was highly selective in what he chose to tell his captives about their current predicament. Swiss units, he reported, were firmly barricaded inside the funicular control buildings at both the top and bottom of the cable. The IOC office had been notified of Melville's situation and was sending representatives.

Bernard did not pass on several other details. The Swiss team manager, a possible pressure point, had been warned after the fact and, wisely, had simply strapped on his skis and taken himself beyond human contact. The authorities converging on the Whiteface parking lot were being assured that delicate negotiations between Melville and Bernard were already in progress. This announcement effectively diminished the possibility of anyone summoning assault troops.

For the IOC members pounding on the unresponsive door of the base station, there were only limited avenues for discharging their pent-up frustration. First and foremost was the loosing of pithy comments at the Swiss reception committee.

"A disgraceful and dangerous perversion of peace-loving pursuits," hissed a Japanese.

"This is never-to-be-sufficiently-condemned hooliganism," thundered a German, reverting to his native rhythms.

A Czechoslovakian had a whole political vocabulary at hand. "Counterproductive and antisocial nihilism," he said.

But it was the Swiss delegate who was suffering the most, as the IOC switchboard forwarded its results. The U.S. member was nowhere to be found, the U.S.S.R. member had disappeared from the face of the earth, the French member had last been seen setting forth—on foot—in search of a lawyer for François Vaux. With just a modicum of luck he, too, could have been among the absent and not faced with these conflicting claims on his loyalty. His appeal to his co-nationals had been loudly hooted down.

"Where was this famous solidarity," demanded Egon, "when you let them disqualify Tilly Lowengard?"

The name was on every lip. In one brief hour she had been enshrined in the same pantheon as Alfred Dreyfus and the Scottsboro boys. On high, Bernard Heise was instructing Anthony Melville about the modern drug culture with an abundance of biting references to Tilly's plight. Below, the gathering mob of athletes, journalists and functionaries reminded itself of what was known about her case. Everyone was talking about her, but where was she? Recognizing an inspiration when it crossed his path, the Swiss member hurled himself at a phone.

And just about the same time as Anthony Melville was experiencing his first qualms of doubt, a jeep deposited Tilly and Dick Noyes at the hub of the controversy. They reacted differently to the sight before them.

Dick took one look at the immobilized cable car and doubled up with laughter. "It's beautiful," he gurgled, "just beautiful."

Tilly, on the other hand, was dismayed. "Oh God," she wailed, "now they'll blame me for this."

Desperately she scanned the crowd until she spotted the familiar faces of two of her disco companions. Pushing her way forward, she clutched imperatively at a sleeve.

"Egon, this is madness. I know you're doing it for me, but you've got to stop. It's dangerous and someone could be—"

"Nonsense, Tilly. You have forgotten how many of

us have worked on the funiculars back home. We are perfectly familiar with the mechanism."

"That's not the point," she snapped at him. "Those are elderly men up there. Anything could happen."

The Swiss delegate was congratulating himself on his acumen, but not for long.

Egon folded his arms, elevated his chin, and transformed himself, if only he knew, into a living replica of Anthony Melville at his most unyielding. "Once and for all, Tilly, you have to recognize that this is bigger than you. This is a matter of principle."

Tilly, too young to realize that these deadly words signaled a posture beyond the reach of persuasion or reason, continued to belabor him with objections. "What about exposure? What if one of them has a heart attack? What if one of them needs pills?"

"All of that has been taken into consideration," Egon rejoined loftily. "There is radio contact in case of a medical emergency. And they are not going to stay up there all night. A settlement will be concluded long before that."

Dick Noyes had stifled his hilarity in deference to Tilly's feelings. Now he threw a consoling arm around her shoulders. "Come on, Tilly, you're working yourself up for no good reason," he urged. "You can count on these guys to do the right thing. Nobody's going to get hurt."

His reassurances were having some effect until Gunther Euler, who had been gleefully circling the base station, flitting from one knot to another, picking up a crumb here and a crumb there, decided to enter the dispute.

"It won't do them any harm to freeze their butts for a couple of hours. Let them see how it feels to be at the mercy of someone else's whims."

In two sentences he managed to offend all three of them.

"We are not operating out of caprice." Egon was stiff as a ramrod. "We are protesting a cover-up. The IOC is deliberately shirking an investigation into how Tilly was really drugged."

Dick Noyes had put behind his initial reaction to Melville's plight. "This isn't fun and games, you know," he said hotly. "Tilly's being railroaded so they can brush the whole mess under the rug, and her reputation is at stake. The public doesn't know what really happened."

As for Tilly herself, she was glaring at the others impartially. "Men!" she raged. "Behaving like little children! Don't any of you have any sense?"

She would have been gratified to know that the two who qualified were the ones actually conducting the negotiations.

Years on the bench had honed Anthony Melville's ability to assess evidence. After being forced to listen to Bernard's exposition, he was profoundly shaken in his assumption of Tilly's guilt. But, in addition to being possessed of an analytic mind, he was also stiff-necked, arrogant and proud of his reputation for toughness. He would willingly subject himself—and his unfortunate companions—to hours of discomfort and real hardship in order to demonstrate his superiority to coercion. It was unthinkable that he should yield to a band of ruffians. It was equally unthinkable that he should connive at trumped-up charges. Stuck on the horns of his dilemma, Anthony Melville badly needed a cogent reason to retreat.

Bernard Heise was intelligent enough to supply one.

As soon as Bernard was convinced that he was making headway on their substantive dispute, he shifted to matters of procedure. "You must understand that we cannot allow this situation to protract itself without offering some public explanation of our conduct," he said soberly. "Of course, the ideal solution would be a statement originating from you. But rather than leave the spectators below in doubt as to what is going on, one of our team, Egon Uhlrich, has prepared an interim release. I would like to read it to you."

As Melville's transmitter necessarily remained off during the next few minutes, Bernard could not hear the mounting crescendo of dissatisfaction greeting his carefully composed sentences. Nonetheless the young Swiss had a fairly good notion of how his words were being received.

"Uhlrich," he said at the end of the reading, "is a law student."

"I might have guessed," Melville retorted.

Egon had produced a small masterpiece. Under cover of the stately impersonal language of a government document, he had gone from a biased account of Tilly's experience to an even more prejudiced recital of the IOC response. But the real damage was in the final paragraph, which left the reader in no doubt as to the motive for this outrageous conduct. Tilly had been drugged by a competitor, and the IOC, more concerned with its public image than with the claims of simple justice, had found it more expedient to brand her a miscreant than to institute a search for the real culprit.

Melville, reduced to gnawing his underlip to a pulp, saw the alternatives clearly. He could stand pat and the Swiss would release this pernicious document. Or he could yield and gain the privilege of describing the confrontation in his own words. Seen in this light, it was no contest.

Bernard was interrupted in mid-flight by the light from Melville's transmitter winking on and off.

"Stop distracting me," the great man ordered. "I'm drafting!"

He was quicker at it than Egon. Within minutes he was reading the finished product to his captor. It was, naturally enough, redolent of the language of the trial courtroom. The world was going to learn that an appeal for a new hearing had been successful. The defense attorneys had brought to the attention of the bench freshly uncovered evidence, the consideration of, which merited *de novo* proceedings. If, in the opinion of the court, these raised a reasonable doubt as to the defendant's guilt, then she would be exonerated and her expulsion from the Olympics rescinded.

"And Tilly gets another run when the slalom continues," Bernard added firmly when Melville concluded.

"Oh, very well. Now see that *this* release gets to the press and burn the other one!"

It was at this point that the limited communication links, thus far so useful to the Swiss cause, began to play merry hell. Melville could talk to Bernard, Bernard could talk to the base station, the base station could talk to the IOC members clustered at its door. When the operator below typed out the release and handed it over to the IOC, it drew a mixed response.

"Thank God," said the German.

"Now we can all go home," said the Japanese, who was cold.

"I will give it to the press," the Czech offered, stretching out his hand.

But Herr Buber, of Austria, shook his head. He continued to frown at the capitulation. "How do we know this comes from Herr Melville?" he objected. "He may not even know about it. We must insist on speaking with him."

There followed a confused babble of suggestion and countersuggestion that soon overflowed onto the airwaves. When Herr Buber grasped the fact that the only radio speaking directly to Melville was on top of Whiteface, he issued a call for expeditionary volunteers.

"It is only a matter of taking the funicular," he reasoned.

More explanations, this time on the counterbalanced nature of aerial tramways. When one car goes up, the other must come down.

"Then we will walk!"

The situation was deteriorating overhead as well. A powerful breeze had developed which, starting with playful buffets, was now imparting to the gondolas a strong, steady oscillation. Already one of the travelers was experiencing the onset of motion sickness.

"What's holding things up?" Melville demanded.

"It's one of your people. He wants to walk up the mountain."

"That's Buber. Pay no attention to him. We never do."

For the first time, Bernard was at a loss. "But there's no way we can convince him that you authorized that communiqué."

"Oh, yes there is! Tell him to look up at the cable car." Melville was stripping a long white scarf from his neck and summoning the aide who was still on his feet. "Here! Flap this out the other window."

He had been galvanized by a sight far below. Perched in his aerie, he could see a long way down the road snaking back to Lake Placid. Coming hell-bent toward Whiteface was an unmistakable television truck.

Nobody knew better than Melville that the network was desperately trying to fill the time originally scheduled for outdoor events. Their trucks were scouring every inch of plowed road for human interest material. (Indeed, they had just passed an exhilarating half-hour with the *Grenoblois* at the Northland Motel. There, memories of check forgery and blizzard conditions had been obliterated by horror at the food provided.) The cable car dangling in the breeze was made to order for television.

Within moments, an alert IOC scout at sea level had also spotted the peril. He raced inside to warn his superiors.

The Czech ripped off a guttural oath. "We had better stop wasting time. Melville has indicated his surrender to us."

"How do we know that was Melville?" Buber asked cunningly. "I say that we should demand assurances—"

The Japanese and the Czech tried to reason with him. The German, recognizing the futility of that course, simply acted. Reaching over when his quarry's attention was distracted, he plucked the release from unwary fingers.

"I will read this to the press," he announced, striding toward the door.

Thereafter Whiteface Mountain, at every altitude, rang with imprecations, commands and entreaties.

"Get this damned thing down," Melville barked.

"Gentlemen, gentlemen! If you will stop firing questions, I have here a statement from the acting head of the International Olympic Committee."

"I still say we should go to the top."

"Start those cameras rolling!" a newsman pleaded. "They're going to move the cable cars."

Victory, such as it was, went to Melville and Bernard. The TV cameras captured nothing more exciting than a tramway proceeding at normal speed. And the news item accompanying this footage merely announced that the IOC was reopening the suspension of Tilly Lowengard.

But a lot of people were able to read between the lines.

At the Andiron Inn they did not even have this raw material to work on. Thatcher, together with Gabler and Hathaway, had been met at the door by Wesley Milliken, who proudly showed them around his operation.

In the billiard room, where two men in shirtsleeves had transformed the table into a command post with annotated index cards arriving at one end and complicated charts emerging from the other, Milliken grinned at Hathaway.

"I'll bet you don't recognize the place. My boys have taken over the dining room and the kitchen, too."

"Just watch it with the refrigerator," Hathaway advised. "I think that's where the tellers keep their beer."

Gabler was impatient with these jocular preliminaries. "I am not altogether clear about your system," he said, leaving no uncertainty as to whose fault that was.

But he had fallen into the hands of a man who reserved his real enthusiasm for work. Domestic jokes were a concession by Wes Milliken to the social niceties. He asked nothing better than to elaborate his methods.

"Of course, we start with general questions. You have to. But on a real slick job, that never helps. Take this situation here in Lake Placid. Most of the depositors begin by saying they can't remember a thing.

This is the busiest two weeks they're going to have in their whole lives. It's standing room only and waiting in line and temporary help everywhere. All they know is the amount they deposited. They don't have a record of denominations or currencies, let alone the names of customers."

His audience nodded gloomily. They had all been in Lake Placid long enough to know what the gift shops looked like during business hours.

"So," said Milliken with unimpaired gusto, "we really get down to cases. We've got an index card for every piece of counterfeit, every depositor, and every name appearing as a payee on a Eurocheck. We start working on every single item, with as much cross-referencing as we need. When you ask specific questions, you're more likely to get answers. Now, I'm not claiming most of it isn't junk but, if you keep at it long enough, the anomalies start popping up. And that's the way you break these setups every time, with the itsy-bitsy little pieces that don't quite jibe."

He had ground to a halt, breathless with the excitement he himself was generating. Thatcher reminded himself to thank the unlucky Quarles back on Wall Street. Quarles might resent having his department raided, but he had given of his best.

"And you've found one of these anomalies?" Thatcher suggested.

"Two of them." Milliken beamed at them. "Tell me how this sounds to you. There's this little restaurant, way to hell and gone. Why in God's name they should be fussier than all the places where you can really run up a tab, I'll never understand. But the Pepper Pot is absolutely certain about its routine. They never accepted one Eurocheck without passport identification. Now, what do you make of that?"

He had hurled the challenge at Hathaway, and Hathaway, after a moment's frowning thought, responded. "It means we've got a lot of innocent people passing phonies. But we already knew that. There was never any guarantee that Bisson's bunch were the only charters who were sold pups right from the start."

"Ah ha!" Milliken cried in triumph. "I knew you'd say that. But listen to what else we've come up with. And that's without getting to the problem of how you persuade a lot of innocents to pass on the same day. We've started talking to the only payees we can identify —the athletes. Well, a German kid hit the roof when one of my boys told him he'd passed a hundred-mark fake. Seems when you talked to him you didn't tell him the denomination. This kid swears he wasn't carrying anything but two-hundred-mark checks. How's that for confusion?"

Hathaway shook his head as if it were buzzing. "That one's harder," he admitted. "I can only think of one explanation. We've got proof that Bisson was careless, and we know he was switching checks in Olympic Village. If he'd make a mistake with his own money, I suppose it's conceivable he didn't match denominations."

"We thought of that one, too," Milliken said approvingly, "but it gets better as it goes on. The kid remembered where he spent money that day and we got hold of the place. There's a clerk who's almost sure she remembers him."

Thatcher did not normally stop the train when it was going where he wanted, but this was so implausible he had to question it. "A clerk in a Lake Placid store says she remembers a transaction five days later? Surely that is suspect. Are you sure she isn't lying?"

Milliken was smug. "She says she doesn't often sell an American Indian headdress to a German."

Even Gabler, constitutionally more suspicious than Thatcher, was silenced by this reasoning.

"Mind you, she won't swear to anything until she gets a chance to see the guy," Milliken cautioned, "but this is the way she tells it. If this is the customer she remembers, he bought a headdress for eighty-five dollars. What's more—and this is the point she's convinced on—he paid with only one Eurocheck."

Three bankers who had the foreign exchange quotes at their fingertips did rapid sums. It was left for Everett to state the obvious.

"A hundred-mark check would only have been worth about fifty-four dollars. He would have had to present two. Therefore the German boy is accurate."

It took more than simple arithmetic to rouse Thatcher. "Good God, that means the substitution took place after the check was at the store. That introduces a whole new dimension to the problem."

As the implications came home to Gabler, he automatically became censorious. "And you haven't arranged a personal meeting between this German and the girl. Good heavens, why not?"

Milliken, too sure of himself to be intimidated, grinned broadly. "Because she hasn't been plowed out. But we'll get to her tomorrow. We've got to. She's heading back to Squaw Valley the minute the Games are over."

"Don't worry, Everett, we'll pin this one down if we have to resort to your snowmobile," Thatcher reassured his subordinate before returning to Milliken. "You certainly seem to be stirring the coals to some purpose. Has anything else come to light?"

"Not yet, but I like the way things are going. I've got my boys doing this by currency. They're finishing up German marks today. Then they'll go on to French francs, then Swiss francs. If that doesn't flush anything, I'll have them—"

His comprehensive plans were interrupted by the entrance of a subordinate.

"Sorry to butt in, Wes, but the IOC is on the phone. They're trying to locate Mr. Withers."

Thatcher's head came up. "So they still haven't found him," he mused. "I'm afraid we can't help."

"They say it's very important."

"I'll bet they do," caroled a new voice. Another shirt-sleeved tabulator had appeared. "I just caught the news. It seems the Swiss team has kidnapped the head of the IOC, and they've got him hanging in a cable car."

"Good God, so that's what he had in mind," exclaimed Thatcher, unconsciously reverting to his last sight of Bernard Heise.

"These crazy kids," marveled Milliken. "There's no telling what they'll be up to next." He was a man of infinite tolerance—except when it came to counterfeiting.

The man who had delivered the telephone message was one of the world's worriers. "I guess the IOC wants Mr. Withers to go over there and take charge, but they'll just have to get along without him."

Thatcher and Everett glanced at each other. Before junior members of the Sloan, Gabler's discipline held firm.

John Thatcher was made of weaker stuff.

"Thank God," he said, "that whatever Brad's up to, he's not doing it in front of television cameras."

172

16 VENUS RISING

BUT while the IOC and the Sloan struggled along without his guidance, Bradford Withers had been overtaken —not to say overwhelmed—by stirring events that were to make their own headlines. Fate had planted him at the skating arena and, for the first hour, he was innocently occupied watching the women's finals.

Vera Darskaya, in red, skated off the ice with an impressive score and an armful of roses. Suzanne Deladier, in white, skated on. Chopin replaced the rock beat that had reminded Brad of happy hours at the disco. But always the gentleman and sportsman, he applauded Suzanne's classic perfection as warmly as he had applauded Vera's vibrant fire. Then, like the rest of the audience, he puzzled over the elaborate scoring system until the computer's decision.

The gold medal was awarded to Vera Darskaya of the Soviet Union.

Suffused in satisfaction, Brad rose. The thrill of individual triumph, the electric response of the gallery, even the poignant droop of Suzanne Deladier's shoulders, all combined to produce that intoxicating distillate of Olympic victory which was a pleasure to inhale. And then . . .

"Mr. Wither-r-r-s! Br-r-adfor-r-d!"

Vera Darskaya, after descending from the platform, had not gone to the dressing room or withdrawn to the sidelines to hold court. She was standing beneath the IOC box, looking up at Withers expectantly.

Puzzled, he reached into his social armory. "Let me be among the first to wish you—"

She interrupted him ruthlessly. "I have considered what you spoke of last night. And now I am acclaimed as a gold medalist, I have decided to go forward!"

Withers, with only the foggiest memory of the previous evening, laboriously dredged up a pertinent detail. "I said you'd be wonderful with the Ice Follies. And if you come over for an engagement, I'm sure you'll be a great success," he added kindly.

"An engagement! Bah!" She dismissed this suggestion at once. "You said that I required creative amplitude, that I could never develop my talents in spiritual fetters."

A gentleman does not contradict a lady, but Withers was fairly confident that he had never used these phrases in his life. Furthermore, if her present performance was any guide, he had never gotten a word in edgewise. He stared at her in mounting horror.

"I am defecting, Br-r-adfor-r-d! I place myself under your protection."

His senses reeled.

"I cannot live without artistic freedom! I am . . ."

Vera Darskaya's voice, ringing with Slavic emotion, had attracted a cloud of bystanders—Olympic stewards, Russian coaches, scavenging journalists. Last, and most reluctant, was the IOC delegate from the U.S.S.R. His attempt to slink out of the building had been foiled by his countrymen.

"Here is Boris Ivanov," cried the coaches. "He will handle this matter."

"Oh, no I won't," he said instantly. "It is not within my jurisdiction."

Withers was quick to seize his cue. "Well, it isn't in mine either," he rejoined.

They glared at each other.

But not for long. As the final cap to their discomfiture, the public address system sprang to life. "Please! We must clear the ice for the pairs events. I must remind the gallery once more against obstructing the skating surface."

There was nothing for it but to move the whole roiling mess backstage, where Withers and Boris Ivanov joined forces in the decision to saddle Anthony Melville with the problem. The plan was splendid, but its implementation proved impossible. The IOC office, wrapped in total confusion, had not informed the girl on incoming calls that a search for missing delegates was in progress. She, under instructions, intoned repressively, "Mr. Melville is not available at the moment."

"Damn the fellow. You can never lay hands on him when you want him," said Withers, blissfully unaware that the clever Swiss had just pulled off that feat.

Boris Ivanov refused to admit defeat. "This is a matter for the civil authorities," he announced. "Let us deliver her to them."

By now Brad was ready to clutch at any straw. Vera Darskaya was hanging heavily on his arm, in spite of all his efforts to detach her.

"Town Hall!" he blurted. "It's just across the street."

So, with Brad and his barnacle leading the way, the parade reformed. They were not received warmly at their destination.

"Who do you people think you're dealing with? Los Angeles?" raved a selectman. "We're just a little town. Our whole Police Department and Fire Department is out at Whiteface because of your president. And that's another thing. Why do you call out our one hook-and-ladder when somebody's trapped hundreds of feet in the air? What good is that supposed to do?"

"Do you mean that Melville is trapped somewhere?" Boris Ivanov asked with a passing flicker of interest.

In Town Hall, Anthony Melville was the man who had exacerbated the ticket debacle. The selectman's account of the Whiteface travail was short and pithy.

"Well, that's too bad," said Brad dismissively. "No doubt they'll get him down sometime. But right now we have to figure out what to do about Miss Darskaya."

"Not with us you don't!"

Vera Darskaya's faith never flagged. She squeezed Withers' arm warmly. "I rely on you completely, Bradford," she trilled with a radiant smile.

Withers turned into a pillar of stone.

Fortunately, Boris Ivanov had been well grounded in the intricacies of American local government before takeoff. "The State of New York?" he suggested, escalating a notch. "Let us communicate with them."

The radiant smile had brought a reporter forward. "Miss Darskaya, will you tell our readers what made you decide to seek asylum?"

"I would never have thought of it myself," she began obligingly. "But last night—"

"And we'll call John Thatcher, too," said Withers desperately.

It had suddenly occurred to him how all this was going to look to his wife, Carrie.

He was luckier than he deserved. Vera Darskaya was strictly a local sensation. Partly this was because the television footage on Anthony Melville was already being processed, partly because of the weather. North America's return to the Ice Age was a hard story to beat. Mostly, however, it was because of the law of diminishing returns. Russian poets, cellists and intellectuals had been flinging themselves at the waiting world at too heady a pace.

Even in Olympic Village, where athletes eddying home from Whiteface and the Arena were bringing the latest news, they were more interested in Vera's performance on ice than off.

"Suzanne skated beautifully," said her youngest teammate with grave loyalty. "It was just that Darskaya was better. Her elevation was fantastic. And her turns—"

Carlo Antonelli tried to curb his impatience. "Yes, I was there, Odette. I saw for myself. But what I want to know is, where is Suzanne now? I tried to find her at the Arena."

"She slipped away early," Odette piped. "And wasn't it exciting about Vera going off with that American?"

Although he knew he was dealing with a child, Carlo could not help asking, "Was Suzanne very upset?"

Odette turned large uncomprehending eyes on him. "Suzanne? She was all right. And even Mademoiselle Gautier says that the judges had no choice."

Carlo was fighting the temptation to shake her when an alternative presented itself. Katarina Maas, suitcase in hand, was sweeping by.

"Thank you, Odette," he said hurriedly. "If you see

Suzanne, please tell her I am looking for her. Now, excuse me . . . Katarina!"

Katarina paused. "Isn't she a little young even for you, Carlo?" she said, with nothing at all uncomprehending about her eyes.

He flushed angrily. "I am looking for Suzanne and I simply wanted to ask if you had seen her," he said, regretting his impulse to hail her.

"Oh?" she said. "I thought you might want to know why I am leaving, or where I am going."

Even amidst his own preoccupations, Antonelli could guess how much this defiance cost her. But criminal or not, Katarina Maas was not playing games in a make-believe world.

"I am sorry, Katarina. I forgot you had your own difficulties," he said quietly.

She bit her lip. "No, I have not seen your precious Suzanne," she snapped, leaving him behind.

But at the doors she was stopped again, this time by brute force. Gunther Euler, storming in, nearly knocked her off her feet.

"Katarina!" he said, grabbing her elbows to steady her. "I am sorry. But I've just come from Intervale. It will be clear tomorrow morning, so we'll be able to jump."

"I am all right, Gunther," she said, disentangling herself. Then, forcing a smile, she added: "I am glad your waiting will soon be over."

He had the grace to look shamefaced. "Oh, I know it doesn't seem like much. But winning this gold medal is important to me, Katarina. I've worked hard for it, and I need it badly. Without it, I have no future. Back to the foundry—that's all. And I don't want to go back to the foundry."

His frankness melted her. "I know," she said. "You

have done a lot to win your gold medal, Gunther. Tomorrow will be your lucky day. I am sure of it."

Euler liked admiration from women, but he wanted no part of Katarina—now. To emphasize the distance between them, he retreated into exaggerated boyishness. "But where are you going?" he cried with an ingenuous smile. "Here, give me your suitcase. I'll take it wherever you want."

Without a tremor revealing that she recognized the rebuff, she said, "The Village has decided that I might sully the purity of Olympic athletes by my presence. So, since the police want me to stay, great effort has been expended to get me a hotel room."

As she spoke, Euler's face darkened. "Crap," he spat. "They're hypocrites, every one of them. They point the finger at others—"

He stopped short, as if she had trapped him into an admission. And before she could reply, their *tête-à-tête* was disrupted.

"Say, has anybody seen where Tilly went?" Dick Noyes demanded. "She was just here."

"No," said Katarina tartly, preparing to leave. "I haven't seen her, either. Gunther, good luck tomorrow morning!"

In fact, Katarina had seen Suzanne Deladier and Tilly not five minutes earlier. They were disappearing into Suzanne's room as she passed. The door had closed behind them with unnecessary speed.

"That awful woman!" Suzanne had exclaimed. "She looks and acts like an expensive call girl. I can't imagine why they ever let her into Olympic Village in the first place."

To the best of her knowledge, Tilly had never encountered an expensive call girl. She had hurried along

179

with Suzanne only to avoid having to talk to Katarina Maas. "I don't know what to say to someone who's out on bail," she confessed.

She was not altogether sure what to say to Suzanne, either. "Suzanne, about your gold medal. I am sorry, but next time you will beat Vera Darskaya—"

"Oh no," Suzanne declared emphatically. "There won't be a next time. I've tried and failed. That is enough."

Tilly, sitting cross-legged on a bed, did not understand the prevailing currents.

Suzanne was detached instead of disheartened. "Darskaya was at her best today," she said, sounding honestly indifferent. "She has a great style. I hope it will be all right for her—this defection to the United States. But you should have seen the look on Mr. Withers' face."

Her unforced giggle made Tilly frown in perplexity. "I thought winning the gold was the only thing you cared about."

Suzanne, who was drifting aimlessly around the room, shook her head. "Oh, no," she said coolly.

Tilly believed her, although she was not sure why. "But, Suzanne, you worked so hard!"

"No harder than you, or anybody else," Suzanne replied. "Since I was here, I decided it was only right to do my best."

"Since you were here?" Tilly echoed. "You make it sound as if they were going to expel you, like they did me."

"Oh, Tilly, I was so glad to hear what happened at Whiteface," said Suzanne. "I know everything will be all right now."

"I think so," said Tilly radiantly. "Most of the committee supports me. So I am here and if I get to compete—I am going to try to win."

"The whole affair was foolish," said Suzanne.

Tilly, glowing with fierce happiness, still wanted to get to the bottom of things. "Yet, now that you've lost to Vera Darskaya, you don't seem to care."

"To tell you the truth," said Suzanne, "it's a great relief!"

"A relief?"

Suzanne looked at her almost shyly. "It has been so complicated. You see, Tilly, nobody expected me to be named to the French team. And last spring, in Rome, I met Carlo. You know, Carlo Antonelli?"

"Yes, I know," said Tilly impatiently. "Go on."

In a rush of words, Suzanne said, "We got married. Oh, Tilly, it was wonderful—but then I was named to the French team and everything seemed completely impossible. You see, I had applied for Italian citizenship. But since Carlo's papa owns a resort at Cortina, Carlo said we could win him over if I skated and got the gold. So we decided to keep it a secret from the committee—that we are married. But, Tilly, it has been so hard! And we have had to take terrible chances, just to be together."

This outpouring left Tilly wide-eyed. "Do you mean that no one knows?" she demanded. "The French team? The Italians? Or the police?"

"No one," said Suzanne. Then, blushing, she added, "No one except Gunther Euler. We had to tell him."

"Why?" asked Tilly bluntly.

But Suzanne was winging away into her own private heaven. "Now we can tell everyone!"

* * *

By the time John Thatcher made a belated appearance at Town Hall, the cast had been enlarged and a new conflict raged.

Front and center was State Police Captain Philip Ormsby, foaming with indignation. "You mean to say this is your idea of an emergency? You called me away from a murder investigation for *this?*"

"What the hell do you expect us to do?" retorted the town representatives. "The selectmen have almost unanimously voted not to become involved."

"So call in a diplomat," rasped Ormsby. "The place is lousy with them. They're in my hair all the time. But why me?"

The selectman was damned if he was going to admit he was acting under Soviet advice. "Because you're listed in the phone book under the State of New York."

Ormsby drew breath for another salvo.

If he was overflowing with anger, Brad Withers was equally distraught. One glimpse of his vice-president, and he was at his side.

"John," he said in anguished tones, "you've got to do something."

Years of practice had made Thatcher adept at winkling unsavory details from his chief. He listened with iron control.

"And now she says she's depending on me to protect her from the Russians," Brad concluded on a woebegone note.

Thatcher cast a skeptical glance at the Soviet contingent. "You can't claim they're resorting to physical violence," he remarked.

The Russians were as far from Vera as they could get, and their indignant comments were aimed at the press.

"As a matter of fact," said Brad, always fair-minded,

"they don't seem to want her back. But they complain that her methods are uncultured."

Thatcher ignored this tempting bypath. "Never mind about that. If they don't want her, what's the problem?"

"Vera says her visa expires with the Games, Vera says she has no place to go, Vera says she's got nothing except what's on her back . . ."

At this point Thatcher acquitted Brad of any ill-advised alcoholic encouragement at the disco. It was Vera who had done all the talking, just as she was doing now with a cluster of reporters.

"Just a moment." Thatcher unceremoniously interrupted the sea of quotations and marched over to the town officials. The selectmen were delighted to exchange Ormsby for a stranger, any stranger.

"You said your vote was almost unanimous. What about the ones who didn't go along?"

The selectman was contemptuous. "Oh, them. They're organizing a committee."

"Thank you." There was genuine gratitude in Thatcher's voice before he wheeled and returned to Withers. "There you are, Brad. The committee can take care of her."

Withers' blue eyes were clouded with apprehension. "Somehow I don't think Vera's going to like that."

Thatcher would unhesitatingly have left Brad to do his own dirty work if there had been the slightest possibility of success.

"But under the circumstances," he said, "it might not be a bad idea if you were to slip away right now."

Naturally it was not that easy. While Brad painfully struggled his way to the right thing to do, Vera caught wind of the committee. A general *éclaircissement* followed which left Vera reproachful but willing to try her wiles on a new target, Brad relieved and bustling down the corridor to search out the committee, and Thatcher ready to depart.

"So they snared you, too." Ormsby, also leaving, was sarcastic. "We're lucky they didn't ring in the President and the Supreme Court."

"I expect they lost their heads for a moment." If Ormsby was unaware of the role played by the Sloan's chief executive, who was Thatcher to tell him? "No doubt they would have come to their senses in a little while."

Ormsby shook his head. "Not if they ever looked up Federal Government in the yellow pages."

If the captain had his way, the State Police would shortly be getting an unlisted number.

"But I'm glad I bumped into you," Thatcher said, trying to look on the bright side. "I've been meaning to call and ask about progress."

Ormsby had fallen into a determinedly bitter outlook. "Well, we've got the police station shoveled out."

Thatcher rose above this gloom. "I mean about Vaux. Did you learn anything from him?"

"God knows he wants to help," Ormsby said dourly. "He'd sell his own mother to buy himself a deal. But he was so nervous about Bisson and the rest spotting him with the Maas woman, he didn't notice much about them. Anyway, I don't think he did."

Thatcher cocked his head. "What do you mean, you don't think?"

Ormsby rubbed his jaw. "By now I'm probably reaching."

"Yes?" said Thatcher inviting him to continue.

"Vaux's been babbling like a brook—but there was just one thing he said that set me thinking. He was talking about Gunther Euler. He got the impression that Euler wasn't really enjoying himself on the snow-mobile outing. That he was just putting up a good show."

Thatcher pondered this. "What's wrong with that? At the time there was a strong presumption that Bisson had the best chance for the gold medal. Euler may have been trying to be a good sport—and not quite succeeding."

"That's what Vaux figures," Ormsby agreed. "But I wonder—maybe Euler spotted Bisson passing that check."

There was a long silence before Ormsby continued. "You see, what worries me is that Bisson, by all reports, was in roaring good spirits the night before he was murdered."

"You mean, *after* the bus trip back?" Thatcher asked, to be absolutely certain.

"That's right," Ormsby said. "Now, if Euler had actually seen the goof, could he have reassured Bisson?"

This was sounding more and more farfetched to Thatcher, and he said so. "Captain, how could anyone have convinced Bisson everything was all right after that fake was passed?"

Ormsby was laboring to construct a reasonable scenario. "By all accounts, Bisson was pretty dumb," he said persuasively. "Maybe he just convinced himself that if nobody had seen his mistake he was out of the woods."

Thatcher did not like to figure as a nay-sayer, but the flaws were too glaring. "But, Ormsby, if nobody saw him and he didn't tell anybody, why isn't he still alive?"

"Yeah," said Ormsby. "There's that."

Thatcher had never found heavy depression conducive to thought. So briskly he said, "You say Bisson was stupid. Do you mean too stupid to have master-minded this counterfeiting?"

"I don't say it's impossible, but it sure as hell sounds unlikely. According to everything I hear, Bisson was more brawn than brains. Maybe he was just playing dumb—but if so, he fooled his teachers back in France, his mother and father, his teammates—"

Thatcher had not been questioning Bisson's capacities. "Then, if he didn't originate this scheme, he must have been recruited. Right?"

Ormsby was willing to go along with that.

"How?" Thatcher asked.

"How? You aren't forgetting that all these people are on the same winter sports circuit," Ormsby reminded him. "They see each other all the time."

"They see each other in a general way. Oh, figure skaters and bobsledders run into each other. But do they get on terms to become accomplices—?"

He broke off, as Ormsby grinned broadly at him. "Have I said anything amusing?"

"They get on terms to marry each other," said Ormsby.

The romance of Suzanne Deladier and Carlo Antonelli, which was roaring through Olympic Village like a forest fire, interested Thatcher.

"They're like Katarina Maas and Vaux," he said. "They were guarding a secret which, presumably, had nothing to do with Yves Bisson's murder. At least it tells us why Miss Deladier—or Mrs. Antonelli—was so unforthcoming when we spoke to her."

"The trouble is that the more information we get, the less we know," said Ormsby, agreeing in spirit.

But Thatcher was not ready for that conclusion. "However, the fact that Deladier and Antonelli knew each other well enough to get married does not destroy my argument."

"Which is . . . ?"

"Which is," Thatcher replied, ignoring Ormsby's skepticism, "that all things considered, Gunther Euler was the one thrown into closest proximity with Bisson over the past few months—or even years."

"My boys have been nosing around," Ormsby told him. "They say the word in Olympic Village is that Euler is a lot sharper than he lets on."

"That can mean anything, can't it?" said Thatcher. "Still, it might warrant taking a closer look at Euler, don't you think?"

As he spoke, Thatcher's thoughts hared off along another line. Intervale was reopening tomorrow morning, which meant, among other things, that time was running out. In days the Olympics would be over.

But Ormsby was thinking about Intervale in other terms.

". . . because it's always possible that the police won't be the only ones taking a bead on Gunther Euler."

17 OUTWARD BOUND

THE Olympics reopened the following morning with cloudless skies smiling down on the crowds gathering at Intervale to watch the ski jumping. Nevertheless, dark shadows remained. Carlo Antonelli was not the only spectator who studied the terrain with Yves Bisson in his mind's eye.

"What's the matter?" demanded Suzanne, openly clinging to him.

"I was wondering how the contestants feel," he said, looking down at her somberly. "Are they expecting a bullet in the back when they jump? Are they worrying about a sniper as they wait up there?"

"Oh Carlo," she cried, "not today! We're here to cheer for Gunther, to enjoy ourselves, to behave like normal people."

"To see and be seen," he said without enthusiasm.

"Why not?" she demanded with a toss of her head. "Are you ashamed?"

"No, no," he said, reflecting how little he really knew Suzanne. The last thing in the world he had expected her to demand was this triumphal procession. The only thing lacking was a bouquet for her to toss.

". . . yes, married all the time," Suzanne was saying to two Canadian girls who had stopped to talk. "Oh, the French were furious when they heard, weren't they, Carlo dear?"

Carlo, wishing himself elsewhere, nodded vaguely, then deliberately turned away to peer at the towers. "I think they're about to begin," he said, but Suzanne was too busy with her friends to pay heed.

Some people had come to watch the jumping. Most of them shared with Antonelli a pang of premonition when the first jumper appeared. Some of them, who were working for Captain Ormsby although they were not in uniform, tensed. But the slim Norwegian landed foursquare on his skis after an unmarred performance. As he coasted nonchalantly to the sidelines, there was a collective sigh of relief.

Needless to say, the true aficionados were thinking technique and nothing else.

"Well, Norway's no threat," announced an expert standing near Antonelli. "He didn't come anywhere near a hundred ten meters."

His companion squinted at the scoreboard which had sprung into electric life. "A hundred eight," he confirmed. "It'll be different when the Germans hit that chute. Keep your eye on Gunther Euler."

A scratch pad with notes was consulted. "Euler's practice was lousy this morning."

"I hope Gunther shows them all," Suzanne, rejoining him, told Carlo in a stage whisper.

To his great relief, the experts simply moved away.

"Gunther has a lot of pressure on him," he said. "Why don't we go closer to the—"

But she willfully misunderstood him. "But, Carlo!

With Gunther's score in the earlier jumps, there are only three others who have any chance at all. Unless he has some sort of accident—"

This was the first time Suzanne had ever lectured him, and Carlo did not much care for it. "Yes, Suzanne. But now, be quiet. Here comes Schecktel from East Germany. He has a strong chance to beat Gunther."

Schecktel's jump stilled conversation until the moment of touchdown.

"Beautiful," murmured the experts, and the scoreboard confirmed them. Schecktel had jumped 113.7 meters.

Carlo turned to make domestic peace only to find Suzanne again enjoying her moment in the sun. While looking on, he too was accosted by a wellwisher.

"Congratulations and all that," said Dick Noyes awkwardly.

"Thank you," said Carlo.

His reserve did not keep Noyes from completing the formula.

"And you're a lucky man, Carlo."

They stood in silence, surrounded by the ebullient crowd, long enough to make Noyes uneasy. Fortunately distraction was at hand.

"It's Gunther!" he and Antonelli said simultaneously.

Euler looked like perfection as soon as he began moving. There was no adjustment in the chute, no discontinuity between being earthborne and airborne, no jerking resolution of the hunched-over tuck into the aerial float high over the heads of the spectators. Gunther simply flowed effortlessly from the starting gate to far, far down the hill.

"Look at him stretch it!" Noyes was reverent.

When Euler landed, beautifully balanced with his elbows barely flared, the cheering began long before the scoreboard announced 114.9 meters. There were five competitors still to come, but that was a formality. The gold medal had been won!

"And so much for all that garbage—about how Gunther wouldn't have a chance if it wasn't for Yves' murder," Dick said robustly. "Yves never jumped like that."

A spectator nearby looked at him sharply. Dick did not notice but Carlo did. With deliberation he said, "Neither did Euler before today. He may be the kind of athlete who needs pressure to perform his best."

"Well, he was just great—whatever the reason," Noyes rejoined.

"Yes," said Carlo, conscious of the eavesdropper. "There can be no quarrel about that."

Certainly not among most spectators who pressed forward to congratulate, to admire, to listen to the answers that the flushed Euler was making for the microphones.

"Yes, this morning I was worried. But as soon as my skis hit the snow, I knew it was going to be better than ever before."

"Well, Gunther, you certainly showed our viewers a wonderful jump. We're looking forward to seeing you again—"

"Oh you will," said Euler, grinning broadly. "You will."

After his bout with the media, he came back to earth with friends and acquaintances crowding around. Like a reigning prince, he began to lead the way from the run-out area, so that remaining competitors could continue. His entourage made a large joyful caravan as they proceeded, and Suzanne, Carlo noticed, had managed to slip in beside the star.

Suddenly, as he and Noyes brought up the rear, all progress stopped.

Gunther was glaring at Suzanne. "What are you talking about?" he demanded in a voice that carried.

Carlo quickened his pace and arrived in time to see Suzanne shrink back.

"B-but, Gunther! We met you at Herr Wennerdonk's! The day after we went snowmobiling. Don't you remember? You saw Carlo and me coming out of the bedroom—"

"What a bride!" he said with an unconvincing laugh. "No eyes for anybody but Carlo! I've never been at any Herr Wennerdonk's. Come on—"

But Suzanne was dug in. "How can you say that, Gunther!"

"I say it because it's true," he said with a flash of naked anger. "Will you please shut your mouth—"

With a muttered oath, Carlo forced his way through the group. Suzanne, after a white-faced glare at Gunther, threw herself into Carlo's arms. He could feel her trembling.

"Carlo," she said against his chest. "Gunther says I am lying. Oh, Carlo . . ."

Over her head, Carlo met Gunther's gaze. "What is all the trouble?" he asked, in a tone that stilled Suzanne.

Gunther was grim. "Your wife says I saw the two of you coming out of a bedroom at Herr Wennerdonk's. She is mistaken, isn't she, Antonelli?"

Blue eyes bored into brown eyes.

"Yes, she must be," said Carlo evenly.

"Carlo!" Suzanne raised her head and stared at him unbelievingly.

"Be quiet, Suzanne," he said, this time with unarguable authority.

Dick Noyes, who had been watching the scene with mounting incomprehension, might have been speaking to them from another world. "Hey, what's going on with all of you?"

"Just a little misunderstanding," said Gunther, resuming his jaunty progress until the public address system thundered.

"At the request of the International Olympic Committee, the announcement of results for the combined ski jumping has been postponed."

Gunther stood stock still, the color draining from his face.

18 DIGGING OUT

ALMOST immediately a flying wedge of stewards rushed up. Before any onlookers could assimilate what was happening, Euler was first isolated, then marched to a waiting car. With sirens blaring, he disappeared from Intervale.

This lightning raid was over almost before it started, leaving behind incredible confusion. Those nearest to Euler had overheard garbled references to "grave charges" and "immediate clarification." By the time they recovered their wits, the public address system was booming non-stop information about the remainder of the day's events—at Intervale, at Whiteface, at the Arena, at the hockey rink.

". . . and at two o'clock this afternoon the final runs of the women's slalom will take place. At eleven o'clock this morning, the biathlon meet . . ."

Meanwhile, the stewards who were not escorting Euler bustled back and began re-establishing order for the next Intervale event, which had been originally scheduled for eight o'clock yesterday, as the loud-speaker declaimed.

The IOC, like John Thatcher, felt the sands of time running out. Only a ruthless push could jam in all the contests dislocated by the blizzard. All over Lake Placid stewards, judges, announcers and timers were on their mettle. They resembled sheep dogs scrambling and barking to keep the slow-witted herd moving in the right direction, to keep stragglers in line.

The governing body, although sedentary, was also hustling along. Under the spur of necessity, Anthony Melville and his distinguished colleagues jettisoned the leisurely procedures so dear to their hearts and began functioning with surgical dispatch.

Gunther Euler was only one of their victims.

Honoring their treaty with Young Switzerland, the IOC had rushed into solemn conclave about Tilly Lowengard first thing in the morning. But these deliberations had been punctuated by rival claims to their attention. Every time one erupted there was a nostalgic stir around the long table, recalling happier pre-deadline days when discussion could flourish unchecked. But Melville bulldozed ahead, reshuffling his notes and reconstructing the docket he proposed to flatten.

"We have to move on. Once we've decided how to handle Tilly Lowengard, we have other issues to face," he said, consulting his watch. There was a heated dispute about a judge's ruling in the hockey match between Finland and Rumania; Czechoslovakia was appealing the penalization of its luge team because the coach had delivered them to the wrong mountain; a poetic English figure skater had finished his stint on the ice by hauling off and socking his coach.

And, according to several informants, *Der Spiegel* was on German newsstands this very morning with an exposé of amateur sports, lavishly illustrated with affidavits, vouchers and photographs proving a covert cash flow between Wennerdonk Sports GmbH and Gunther Euler.

Before the blizzard, this appalling roster would have consumed days. But realism had set in with a vengeance, even in the unlikeliest breasts.

"It's sad but true," said Bradford Withers heavily. "We simply can't give these matters the scrupulous attention they deserve."

Melville was dishing out justice, summary or not. "We'll have to have Euler in, to see if he has any vestige of a defense. I think we should be ready to announce our decisions in about an hour!"

They were ready in exactly thirty-five minutes.

Melville read the official document to the very few members of the press who had managed to make it in time.

". . . reaching a consensus of opinion," he droned. There was not one squeak of protest from his brethren who flanked him with the sobriety appropriate to a summit. Consensus had been there all the time; draping it in unobjectionable language was what had detained them. "The IOC has decided . . ."

To nobody's surprise, the IOC endorsed all its officials and their rulings, defended regulations even where athletes were blameless, and declined to exercise intra-team jurisdiction.

Melville moved on to more controversial areas with the same colorless prose. ". . . Miss Mathilde Lowengard. Medical and other evidence exonerate her completely from the charge of having recourse to substances prohibited by Olympic rules. Accordingly, her suspension is hereby lifted and Miss Lowengard will be permitted to compete in the women's slalom this afternoon."

A smoker's cough from the back of the room made him glare as if tumult had broken out.

"About Gunther Euler," he resumed. "We have confronted Mr. Euler with the allegations carried in a current periodical. Mr. Euler cannot—and does not—deny them. There is therefore no doubt that he has forfeited his amateur status by accepting payment for activities as an athlete. The IOC has no alternative but to expel him from this Olympics. The gold medal in the combined jump will be awarded at this evening's ceremony to Bruno Schecktel from East Germany. Finally, I am happy to announce that weather conditions now permit the resumption of all events. Thanks to the unremitting efforts of the staff, the cooperation of local authorities . . ."

No matter how Melville camouflaged them with ground crews and trail groomers, Tilly and Gunther Euler were news. And in Lake Placid, news was moving considerably faster than traffic.

Olympic Village had learned about his expulsion long before Gunther set foot over the threshold. The embarrassed silences, the averted eyes, the halfhearted waves that greeted him were more eloquent than words. Euler hesitated and, quite suddenly, the blinkers of impotent fury fell from his eyes.

"Fantastic!" he said to himself, resuming his walk. "From a gold medal to a public spanking, all within an hour!"

The familiar surroundings of Olympic Village only heightened the contrast, the irony, the absurdity of the extremes.

Gunther preferred to forget the proceedings between acclaim and disgrace. By the time he finished showering, he had managed to do so. The unnerving shock of the IOC's swooping descent, his own stupefaction at *Der Spiegel*'s facts and figures and—worst of all—his childishly sullen collapse under questioning first faded, then evaporated.

Euler was whistling as he sauntered downstairs to show the world that he was himself.

All the turbulence outside filtered inexorably into the Sloan's branch in Olympic Village. Everybody who dashed in to cash a check or buy a money order stayed to gossip. John Thatcher and Everett Gabler, working at a desk near the railing, were kept fully abreast of breaking events.

But here, too, the specter of a deadline was honing cutting edges.

"Euler?" Everett repeated brusquely. "The only German athlete in whom I have the remotest interest, Hathaway, is the purchaser of this . . . what was it? . . . this Oswego Indian headdress. With what appears to have been an authentic Eurocheck. John . . . ?"

"Milliken is downtown, talking to the salesgirl at this very minute," said Thatcher firmly. "But you do remember, don't you, Ev, that they're just beginning to tally German and French Eurocheck holders against the varied counterfeit denominations we've been landed with."

"High time!" Gabler snorted, returning to his long, unrewarding lists.

With peace restored in that quarter, Thatcher turned to Roger Hathaway. What he saw, reasonably enough, was resentment. Nobody enjoys snubbing dismissal of his conversational coin.

"The IOC's fine distinctions about amateurism elude me, although I gather Euler overstepped the mark," said Thatcher, laying down a pencil to indicate readiness for a brief break. "But I am glad to hear about Tilly Lowengard. It would be a shame if she weren't allowed to race. When is it?"

"First thing after lunch," said Hathaway shortly. Then, with a smoldering look at the oblivious Gabler, he said, "Well, I'd better keep an eye on the tellers. Unless there's anything I can do here."

"Not at the moment," said Thatcher, with an inward sigh. His regret did not stem from the impasse that was turning Everett so tetchy, but from his own executive shortcomings. When push comes to shove, when the day of reckoning approaches, when the curtain is about to fall, the man-at-the-top has one supreme responsibility—to keep his troops from falling apart.

Thatcher feared that he was not pulling it off. These were countdown days with athletes and everybody else preparing to leave Lake Placid. Each passing moment increased the possibility that the whole Eurocheck swindle might go unpunished. Everett was growing more fractious. Hathaway, already under strain, could barely meet the demands of current Sloan operations.

Only Milliken and his band of specialists were happy as beavers with their incessant, meticulous work. And from where Thatcher sat, it did not look as if their dam would be finished in time.

He sighed again and attracted Everett's attention.

"Come up with something, John?" he said alertly.

"Not yet," said Thatcher, diving into another one of Milliken's immensely detailed master lists.

For a short period they worked in silence amidst the cheerful hubbub of young people swirling in and out of the bank. Then the orchestration changed and Thatcher realized that he was being singled out.

"Mr. Thatcher! In case we do not see you again, I

want to say au revoir. Suzanne and I are leaving this afternoon for Rome."

Thatcher rose to greet the Antonellis and wish them well. Suzanne, with her cheeks still rosy from the cold, with a furry hat framing her face, was pretty as a picture. And, Thatcher suspected as he concluded his courtesies, she knew it.

Meanwhile her husband was chatting without a care in the world. "I was lucky to get tickets to Rome," he said. "Since it is not too easy to make reservations these days, we thought we'd better skip the closing ceremonies. Besides, with the French team being so disagreeable about Suzanne, I am not sorry to be leaving this Olympics. In fact . . ."

His remarks might have continued indefinitely but suddenly awareness cut through the bank, freezing everybody in place. Like a figure out of an old-fashioned Western (and Thatcher later decided that the Oswego headdress had summoned this image), Gunther Euler filled the doorway.

Then he located what he wanted. In two long strides, he joined Carlo, Suzanne and Thatcher.

"They told me you were in here," he said heartily.

Suzanne glanced imploringly at her husband.

"Gunther, I . . . and Suzanne, too . . . we are both sorry you were disqualified," Antonelli said. "And I hope you believe that neither of us had anything to do with it."

With a deep laugh Euler reassured him. "No, no. That was reporters, always out for dirt. Well, *Der Spiegel* found it, and who cares?"

He looked down at Suzanne benevolently. "So I've come to apologize. You understand how it was, don't you, Suzanne?"

"No, I don't," she said with asperity.

It was Carlo who explained to her. "Wennerdonk's, Suzanne," he said. "Where we saw Gunther."

When Suzanne nodded, Thatcher allowed himself a significant *ahem*.

"Of course, you weren't there," Carlo remembered. In a few carefully chosen words he described to Thatcher the squabble about the ski chalet rented by Wennerdonk Sports GmbH.

All this discretion was wasted.

"Wennerdonk's is where I never should have been at all," said Gunther unrepentantly. "Not when I have my . . . er, arrangement with them. So I said you were mixed up, Suzanne. I thought I had to. But now it turns out that *Der Spiegel* already knew. So it was all a waste of time. And I hope you forgive me."

He put the full force of his personality into a winning smile.

"Of course I forgive you," she cried warmly. "And I just wish that . . . that . . ."

"That the IOC didn't take away my gold medal this morning?" he finished for her. "Don't worry about it! I am still the best ski jumper in the world and everybody knows it. Nothing these old men do can change that! I'm all right!"

Thatcher wondered if Wennerdonk Sports GmbH would take the same view. The commercially desirable golden lad does not solicit under-the-table payments.

". . . so they do not worry me at all. And I told them so to their faces," Euler continued, grandly pulling out a bulging wallet. "I have what I came here for, and now I'm ready to go. I'll have to cash some checks . . ."

As Euler continued his challenge to the world, Carlo Antonelli grew restive. "Well, good luck, Gunther," he interrupted, taking Suzanne by the arm. "We've got things to do before we leave. We told you we're flying to Rome, didn't we?"

Euler watched them depart. "The happy bride and groom," he said, half under his breath. "Between you and me, I don't envy Carlo."

Thatcher, holding his tongue, wondered. Gunther Euler might not want a young —and to all appearances spoiled—wife. But how did an indulgent family, an exclusive ski resort in Cortina, look to him?

Euler could have heard the question, unspoken though it was. "Everything Carlo's got, papa gives him," he said matter-of-factly. "My father works in a foundry."

Then, as if regretting this self-revelation, he turned to business. "So, I'm cashing a check. Will four thousand American dollars be all right . . . or should I wait until I get to New York? I'm going to be staying with friends, but we'll be going out a lot. Of course I've got credit cards, but I feel better with enough cash."

A trumpet would not have been more effective. Gunther had his audience back, in no way diminished. Carlo and Suzanne had left, but this showy display of wealth drew all eyes, including Everett's.

"You did say Milliken was just starting on the German marks, didn't you?" he hissed in Thatcher's ear.

But Hathaway was all business.

"Four thousand is fine," he said, extending his hand for Euler's checks and signaling a teller.

When the cash duly appeared Euler could not resist a dig.

"Maybe I do all those bad things that the IOC gets so uptight about . . . but at least the checks I give your bank are good."

While Everett Gabler quivered beside him, Thatcher felt a pang of sympathy for this young giant. He had

202

everything to fulfill the Olympic ideal of gentlemanly amateurism, everything except money.

"No, despite what the IOC says," Euler continued, "I haven't been the worst person here at the Olympics. Compared to the rest—"

He broke off and swiveled to face the door.

"Tilly!" he roared, spreading his arms wide.

19 RADIATIONAL COOLING

TILLY Lowengard came bouncing past the writing tables with Dick Noyes, her eyes shining. After hugging Gunther, she scanned the long lines of customers. Thatcher could tell she was looking for an excuse to shout her good tidings aloud.

"Bernard! I've been cleared to race!" she yodeled joyfully the length of the bank.

Bernard Heise, who was just finishing up with a teller, stuffed his money into a wallet, smiled broadly and strolled back to join Tilly at the end of the line. His arrival was a relief to Dick Noyes, who was finding Gunther a major embarrassment.

Tilly, however, was riding such a wave of happiness that she had soared beyond the reach of social pinpricks. "Oh Gunther," she cried. "I'm so sorry it didn't work out for you, too." Today she wanted a world in which everyone felt as wonderful as she did.

Faced with this exuberance, Gunther Euler proved his claim to at least one facet of the Olympian spirit— the ability to take pleasure in someone else's triumph.

Leaning down to kiss her cheek, he said steadily, "I am, too, but better one casualty than a whole bunch. And don't worry about me, Tilly," he added. "I got my chance to show them what I can do."

Dick, casting around for another subject, spied the knot of bankers and recognized a diversion.

"Say, Roger!" he called. "And Mr. Thatcher! Did you know that Tilly had her hearing this morning and everything's okay now?"

Thatcher said he was very pleased, Hathaway stoutly maintained he had never doubted the result and Everett summoned a wintry smile in honor of the occasion. Thatcher then decided that, in this orgy of felicitation, there was one further accolade to bestow.

"I understand this is all your doing," he said to Bernard Heise.

"Oh, yes. I wouldn't even be here today, if it wasn't for Bernard and Egon," Tilly chimed in eagerly. "It's a shame they weren't with me this morning. It was really their victory."

Bernard's zeal for tactics had not been exhausted by Whiteface.

"I would have enjoyed it," he said, admitting weakness, "but we didn't want any last-minute hitches. I knew Melville would back down more readily if I wasn't there. And Egon, thank God, is in the fifty-kilometer cross-country today."

"Just as well," grinned Dick Noyes. "Melville seems able to swallow you, but the mention of Egon still turns him purple."

This came as no surprise to Bernard, who shook his head disapprovingly. "I told Egon to forget about that brief he wrote. But nothing would stop him from shoving it at Melville after the cable car was down. Egon honestly thought he was going to get it printed some-how."

"Get what printed?" Tilly asked a second before Thatcher could.

Gunther and Dick both felt she had missed one of life's joys. "Didn't you ever get a chance to read it?" they demanded.

Tilly reminded them that the IOC delegates had rushed her into seclusion as soon as they had regained control at Whiteface Mountain. It had been part of Melville's policy for downplaying the publicity value of the Swiss confrontation. No dangling gondolas to photograph, no pretty girls to interview, no inflammatory press releases to publish.

"Egon did a beautiful job," Gunther murmured. "Even I could tell that much. You would have loved it."

Bernard had no use for futile regrets. "Egon thinks he can reform the world all at once," he said dispassionately. "Things don't work that way. We must proceed step by step. But this time Egon is being stubborner than usual. He must know that release has served its purpose."

John Thatcher had more experience with bright young men than Bernard Heise, and he realized that this was not a case of misplaced idealism. Egon was fired by the enthusiasm of the creative artist; he was infatuated with his own masterpiece. He could not bear to think that something so beautiful, so perfect, so supremely well-tailored to the immediate need, should be discarded.

Dick Noyes took a simpler approach. "Egon's mad at the whitewash, and I don't blame him. You weren't there, Bernard, but you should have seen the way Melville acted today when it was all over. He was patting

Tilly on the shoulder, beaming paternally at her and welcoming her back aboard. Naturally it was so wonderful, we were pleased. But when you think about it, that old fox has gotten everything his own way. There wasn't one word about finding out who drugged Tilly and disqualifying *her*. That would make too much of a stink. But Melville doesn't mind draping medals on some girl who wins the slalom by passing out Mickeys."

"Wait a minute." Tilly had been looking first at Bernard, then at Dick in confusion. "Was Egon claiming that someone in the slalom drugged me?"

"Of course he was." Dick had worked himself into a welter of indignation. "Look, Tilly, I know you've been too busy trying to undo the damage to wonder who was responsible. But whoever she was, she's going to get away with it, and I say that's a crying shame."

Tilly was serenely confident. "You're all wrong. I know the girls who are competing, and none of them would do something like that."

Dick immediately said that Tilly was too trusting for her own good. He was supported by Bernard, who urged Tilly not to underestimate the depravity of others.

Thatcher, on the fringes of the controversy, was struck by the warmth with which the boys continued to press their conviction. Why did they assume they knew better than Tilly? By all accounts she had been on the international circuit for three or four years. Dick was the merest tyro and even Bernard was a latecomer. The only one who could claim his experience outclassed hers was Gunther Euler. And Gunther, Thatcher suddenly realized, was frowning heavily and not volunteering one single word.

Moved by genuine curiosity, Thatcher edged over to

the ski jumper. "You're the veteran, Euler," he said in an undertone. "What's your opinion? Would most competitors act that way?"

Euler hesitated. But when he spoke, there was nothing indecisive about his words. "Take drugs themselves . . . yes. But feed them to someone else? Absolutely not."

The adversaries, meanwhile, had not succeeded in budging each other an inch. Tilly insisted that she knew the people involved. Bernard had theories about the underside of life. And Dick informed both of them that he was the one with his feet on the ground.

"Because you've got to face facts, Tilly," he said. "Somebody had to have a reason for drugging you, and it sticks out a mile what that reason was."

"If we're going to talk about facts," she retorted instantly, "nobody in the slalom had a chance to do it."

"You can't be sure of that. It was days ago."

Tilly, whose blood was up, had no qualms about sweeping Roger Hathaway into the dispute. "You remember, don't you, Roger? We had lunch in the cafeteria and we sat with Gunther and Dick."

As befitted a banker, Hathaway qualified his reply. "I remember lunch," he admitted cautiously, "but you could have bumped into anyone before."

"You see, Tilly!" Dick was almost crowing. "You don't know when you got the stuff."

"But I do! The doctor told me all about the results of the analysis. And he says I would have been feeling the effects within thirty to forty minutes."

Dick was looking more and more like a baffled bull. Well, thought Thatcher unsympathetically, he was the boy who had wanted to deal in facts. If they were unpalatable, he had only himself to blame.

"That just doesn't make sense," Dick complained.

"Nobody knew where you were going to eat. Are you trying to tell me that somebody was wandering around with a bunch of knockout drops?"

"Not knockout drops. The doctor said it was a type of allergy medicine. Probably a double or triple dose." Tilly, who had been so positive until now, faltered. "It seems some people carry it around all the time."

Her confusion, Thatcher decided, was a tribute to rampant good health. A bodily ailment, in her life, was a broken leg or a twisted shoulder. Of course Tilly knew, in a vague academic way, that the world was filled with asthmatics, diabetics, epileptics. Nonetheless the simple statement that certain individuals routinely carried medication opened vistas that seemed to her outlandish. Thatcher found this naivete rather endearing. As for Everett Gabler, whose whole existence was a battle to avoid offending his stomach, he looked downright envious.

"I suppose you wouldn't have any tolerance for this medicine," Thatcher remarked to her. "Particularly for an overdose. That would certainly explain your reaction."

"The doctor said I was suffering from an acute case of antihistamine drowsiness," Tilly quoted as if by rote. "He said I was lucky I didn't crash into a tree."

Her calm was raising Dick's hackles. "Listen, I want to make sure I've got this straight. The doctor claims the stuff had to go into you at lunch. But, Tilly! You had lunch with me and Gunther. I remember calling to you and Roger as soon as you got off the line and you came straight over."

Before anybody could explore the appalling implications of this remark, Roger Hathaway coughed compellingly. They all turned to stare at him.

"I think you might expand lunch to lunchtime," he

suggested. "Tilly pushed that tray from one end of the counter to the other, and she stopped a number of times to say hello to people. In fact I remember waiting for her at the end while she was finishing up with that Italian."

"Carlo Antonelli," Dick supplied instantly.

It was all coming back to Tilly. "You're right," she agreed. "And I wished Suzanne luck in the school figures, too."

There was an uneasy silence.

"I suppose you could say," Tilly continued reluctantly, "that the people who were near my tea were the same ones who went snowmobiling at Saranac."

Privately Thatcher thought that was an overly polite way of describing them. You could also call them the group suspected of murdering Yves Bisson.

That, in any event, was how it struck Dick Noyes. "Jesus Christ!" he roared loudly enough to rivet the entire bank. "I've been thinking this police malarky was a joke until now. But somebody *did* shoot Yves and, if the same guy is after you, Tilly, you're in danger."

"Now don't exaggerate," she said with an edge to her voice. She had rattled herself enough not to welcome any intensification. "A couple of harmless pills isn't the same thing as killing someone."

"I didn't say it was, but it's still no joke."

"You don't have to tell me that! I'm the one who went down Whiteface half unconscious."

If Dick had been more experienced, he would have been warned by the rising note. Instead he plunged doggedly on. "Well, thank God the IOC hearing is over. Now there's nothing to keep you here. You can simply clear out."

"I'd have to think about that, I don't know how it

would look," Tilly said irritably. "Nobody leaves right after they race."

"What's to think about? We agreed you were going to visit my folks in Colorado as soon as the Games were over. You'd just be going a little early. And I don't mean tonight, I mean now—on the next bus."

Tilly could not believe her ears. "Dick, the slalom starts in two hours."

"To hell with the slalom! That's how you got clobbered last time. Suppose this weirdo decides to use cyanide this time?"

"You're not serious. I worked to get to Lake Placid for three years, and so far, what have I got to show for it? First I look like a clown on the slope, then I get thrown out in disgrace. Today, things are going to be different."

Dick was leaning over her as if he wanted to ram his argument down her throat. "I'm not talking about how you look on TV," he shouted, beginning to wave his hands. "I'm talking about your life. Can't you get that through your fool head?"

"You may be convinced I'm in danger, but I'm not. And don't call me a fool!"

"Well, you're acting like one! Which is more important—your safety or some tinpot medal?"

Tilly's eyes narrowed to slits. "That medal wouldn't be so tinpot if you had ever stood the slightest chance of winning one."

"Wonderful!" Dick spat. "So now I'm supposed to be jealous of you as a skier."

Thatcher and Gabler had instinctively faded back several paces, only too grateful to let the tide of bank business sweep Tilly forward to the teller and out of their immediate vicinity. Bernard and Hathaway had not been quite so agile and they paid the penalty.

Bernard, proving his dedication once again, even ventured into the arena. "Now, Tilly," he said ponderously, "it doesn't make any difference how badly Dick skis. You should listen to him, he's making sense."

"Just twenty-four hours ago you were telling me that my being in the slalom was so vital it excused kidnapping and hijacking. Now, when it's what *I* want to do, it doesn't matter at all. Why should I listen to someone who can't make up his mind?" Tilly demanded, plunking a traveler's check under the grille.

Bernard bit his lip. "I can make up my mind," he retorted, making the fatal error of justifying himself. "Yesterday was a matter of principle."

"Ha!" bleated Tilly. "Well, today it's my principle."

The teller, who had been vainly trying to attract Tilly's attention by flourishing a neat packet of bills, abandoned sign language. "Your Eurocheck is quite valid," he announced in stentorian accents.

"You're damned right it is," said Tilly, reminded of old grievances. "And so was the last one I cashed here, no matter what anyone says!"

But the teller, unlike so many of his contemporaries, had dealt with the great American public. "Yes, miss," he mumbled in such an impersonal, disembodied voice that Tilly might just as well have tangled with a recording. Abandoning him in search of worthier prey, Tilly swung on Roger Hathaway.

"And I suppose you think Dick's making marvelous sense, too," she dared him.

One glance at her white pinched face was enough for Hathaway. "I agree you ought to leave, but I don't see that a couple of hours makes all that much difference."

Thatcher wished that the branch manager had as

much sense as his teller. He should have foreseen that pacifying Tilly would enrage Dick.

Sure enough, Dick came barging in. For the next five minutes an astonishing number of charges and countercharges hurtled through the air. Hathaway's departure from competitive skiing after college, in Dick's eyes, debarred him from encouraging anyone to race.

"You didn't think it was so all-important."

Dick's assumption that Colorado and Whiteface were Tilly's only alternatives was labeled a monstrous piece of egotism.

"I can always go back to Interlaken, to my job at the bank!"

Bernard's ill-considered plea that they should all remain calm and discuss this like civilized beings almost brought Hathaway down on him.

But if the men had unlimited time for these pyrotechnics, Tilly did not. She had to change, to catch the bus to Whiteface, to take the lift to the waiting area.

"And that's what I'm going to do," she said roundly. "If you want to see me, you know where to find me. If you don't want to see me, that's all right too!"

Her exit was living proof of the powers of femininity. In spite of heavy boots and a cumbersome down jacket, she produced a flounce that could not have been bettered in a bustle.

Dick Noyes stared at the closing door, then transferred his embittered gaze to his companions. Gunther Euler, who had prudently sidelined himself during the hostilities, offered a bromide about tension immediately prior to competition. This was apparently the final straw. Dick took a deep breath, prepared to blast him to smithereens, then abruptly ran out of steam.

"Oh hell!" he said to no one in particular before he too stormed out of the bank.

As peace descended, Roger Hathaway returned to his superiors. "Whew!" he said feelingly. "Dealing with these wildcats makes you glad to get back to banking."

Thatcher could see a lecture taking shape on Everett Gabler's lips, and an unfair one at that. It was not Hathaway's fault that Sloan customers should choose the bank, out of all the amenities provided in Olympic Village, for their domestic spats.

"We could all profitably get back to business," he said hastily.

Hathaway was right with him. "If there's nothing more I can do for you, I'd better check out the downtown branches."

"Splendid," said Thatcher, speeding him on his way. "And, Everett, defer your indignation for a moment. I want to talk about something else. Were you paying attention to what Noyes was saying?"

"Of course I was," Everett rejoined. "With the Antonellis and Euler virtually cleared, the Saranac party reduces to Noyes and Tilly Lowengard. And, in spite of your earlier suspicions, Miss Lowengard is not seizing excuses to leave Lake Placid."

Thatcher was more troubled than he cared to admit. "No, but Noyes is remarkably anxious that she should. He started out by trying to tie the drugging to a competitor. When that didn't work, he shifted with remarkable promptitude into the effort to have her depart."

Everett liked to lay out all possibilities. "It could be genuine solicitude."

"Of course it could. But why these attacks on Tilly in the first place? None of these young people suggested so much as a hint of a reason."

Everett snorted. "Naturally. They are incapable of rational thought."

"Rational or not, Noyes may have kept his eye on

the ball. If the girl is in danger, her protection is the immediate concern."

"Are you suggesting that we prevent her from eating and drinking? How can we? That isn't our province."

"No, it isn't." Thatcher had made up his mind. "But it is Ormsby's. I think the police had better take a hand."

20 FROST HEAVES

WHAT Thatcher required was a phone and privacy.
The Sloan in Olympic Village offered the first, but not
the second. In theory, discreet conversations could be
conducted under cover of the pervasive clatter. But
Thatcher was wise in the ways of applied acoustics;
the minute he reached Captain Ormsby, the bank would
fall silent as a tomb. Since he did not want his comments reverberating through the whole compound, he
set off for the pay phones in the main lobby.

Ormsby was not happy when he heard what Thatcher
had to say.

"My God, I read all about her being kicked out. Now
you're telling me that somebody may have been trying
to shut her up. How long have those stuffed shirts at
the IOC known about this? And why the hell didn't
they report it?"

Tempers were getting short at the police station too,
Thatcher realized. "I think they just got the complete
analysis this morning," he said.

"And never put two and two together," Ormsby

groaned. "Well, that kid's going to have a long talk with me about everything she knows, or thinks she knows."

Thatcher was sorry to have to carp. "She's racing this afternoon."

But Ormsby's blood was up. "I'll send a couple of my boys to Whiteface, and they'll pick her up the minute she hits the finish line."

Well, that took care of where Tilly Lowengard would be eating and drinking tonight, Thatcher thought as he hung up. Now he could turn his attention to what he himself would be doing along those lines.

"Everett," he said, upon returning to the bank, "let's have lunch."

"So long as it isn't the cafeteria," said his loyal subordinate.

Any cafeteria was penance for Gabler. The rich profusion of dietary abominations, the mountains of saturated fats, the carbohydrates heaped on carbohydrates —all these offended his purist's soul, as if his chaste cottage cheese could be contaminated by its neighbors. But at Olympic Village it was the trays that staggered him, not the steam tables. Watching hungry young athletes stoke up left him aghast.

"Pizza, chop suey, french fries, followed by two helpings of banana pie and chocolate ice cream!" he had choked during their one and only visit. "They're poisoning themselves."

"If anything, they're too healthy," Thatcher replied as Gabler repeated the sentiment.

"In view of the virtually non-stop spectacles we have witnessed here this morning," said Gabler, rising to follow Thatcher, "I am inclined to suspect some sort of chemical imbalance."

"It's called youth," said Thatcher, leading the way. "Come along, Ev."

The Beefeater, which they reached ten minutes later, was a welcome change from Olympic Village and its distractions. The menu was severely limited and, even under the pressure of incessant crowds, the atmosphere was sedate.

There was, however, the unavoidable wait for a table. Thatcher was idly inspecting the glass shelves of the lobby gift shop when he was reminded of an obligation.

"What I'd really like to take back to Miss Corsa is an Oswego war bonnet," he mused. "But perhaps I can find something in here."

Everett held his peace. He himself belonged to an older and perhaps better school. Each Christmas he presented his secretary with an extremely expensive gift of impeccable good taste and dullness. This annual rite was sufficient for him, but not for Thatcher. Each year the whole transaction struck Thatcher as about as pleasurable as a second mortgage.

So he had fallen into the additional habit of bringing Miss Corsa souvenirs of his various travels. And, as witness the Oswego war bonnet, he allowed himself considerable latitude. This practice afforded him much innocent enjoyment.

Gabler, who did not have a playful bone in his body, followed Thatcher into the gift shop, recoiling slightly under the lethal fumes of massed scented candles.

"It doesn't look promising," said Thatcher, agreeing in spirit. Besides scented candles, there were innumerable small carved animals, whimsical aprons and potholders, jars of misguided jams and ornamental baskets. None of these fired Thatcher's imagination, and he was about to leave brass paperweights behind when he was accosted.

"Mr. Thatcher! This doesn't mean something's wrong after all, does it?"

Her hair was white, her eyes were blue and her smock was bright green. She dropped a raffia placemat and projected enough fluttering anxiety to unnerve Thatcher.

"I mean about Eurochecks," she said as he stooped to retrieve her stock. "Oh, thank you. I'm Mrs. Talley. Of course, I know who you are. I guess just about everybody in Lake Placid does. But I'm afraid . . ."

Smiling piercingly, she gazed at Everett. The high social manner was so overpowering that Thatcher found himself performing introductions.

"I'm so glad to meet you," Mrs. Talley said graciously. "But I do hope this doesn't mean that charming young teller of yours was wrong. I can't tell you how we've been crossing our fingers since we heard that counterfeit checks have been circulating. Because we've been doing quite a lot of business with people from overseas. They all love the Beefeater, and I must say, I think it's one of the better restaurants in the area, don't you? But there's always a wait and a lot of people don't care to sit in the bar—particularly at lunch . . ."

This flow might never have ended if Gabler had not taken a hand.

"Eurochecks? And our charming young teller?" he said, with his talent for separating wheat from chaff.

"Oh yes, she's really delightful," Mrs. Talley trilled right back at him. "You must be proud of your staff here in Lake Pacid. They've all been so helpful and polite."

"I'm delighted to hear it," Thatcher murmured, but Gabler was made of sterner stuff.

"Do I understand that one of our tellers told you that something was wrong with the Eurochecks you've been accepting?" he asked suspiciously.

"Oh no!" she cried. "She came in just about an hour ago. And she told me that you've looked over all our receipts—and they're all good. I was simply overjoyed. That's why I was so worried when I saw both of you gentlemen. Because, as I said, I knew that you have a very important position at the Sloan, Mr. Thatcher. I'm afraid I didn't recognize you, Mr. Grabber. Because, if there's one thing we don't need right now, it's all this aggravation. Oh, the Olympics have been wonderful for all of us, but it's been hectic as I'm sure you can see. Why, would you believe . . ."

Drastic measures were called for, and Thatcher unhesitatingly took one.

"Mr. . . . er, Grabber and I have to be getting on to lunch. But before we go, I believe I'll take this salt-and-pepper set."

"I'm sure your wife will adore it," said Mrs. Talley instantly, naming a price. Exorbitant though it was, it got them out of her clutches and back into the lobby. But before they could proceed into the dining room, Thatcher halted.

"Would you mind postponing lunch, Ev?" he asked.

"Not in a good cause," said Gabler stoutly. "What did you have in mind?"

"Something that woman said, oddly enough," Thatcher replied. "Come on, and we'll commandeer transport to Saranac. I'll explain on the way."

By great good fortune, they emerged from the restaurant just in time to see a minibus shuttle pulling up. Even better, it was not filled to overflowing.

"The density's lessening in these last days of the Olympics," said Thatcher, choosing a seat and carefully placing the salt-and-pepper set beside him where he could most easily forget it. "The Antonellis aren't the only people who are going earlier than might have been expected."

"Here, you'd better let me hold that, John," said Gabler. "Otherwise you're sure to leave it behind when we reach Saranac. Now, will you tell me why we're going there?"

"Mrs. Talley told us that a Sloan teller said that her Eurochecks were all right. Well, that set me thinking. Ormsby and I have been wondering who knew that Yves Bisson passed a counterfeit check at Twin Forks. We concluded that it was one of his companions there —or somebody he himself told. But before he was murdered, there was somebody else who knew—somebody in the Saranac bank. You recall that the counterfeit surfaced in Saranac. It wasn't until after Bisson was murdered that Roger Hathaway got busy and discovered what we had in our vaults. Now, to the best of my knowledge, nobody has explored this avenue. It's an outside possibility, but I think the people in Saranac bear interviewing."

Gabler listened intently, then nodded. "Better not to leave any stone unturned," he said, speaking more prophetically than he knew.

Mr. Pomeroy of the Saranac Trust and Savings was granitic in every way. When his secretary ushered distinguished conferers from New York City into his office, he was studying Thatcher's card without enthusiasm. "The Sloan, eh? Well, what can I do for you?"

This attitude was not only unpromising, it was unexpected. On the whole, cordiality obtains between one bank and another. Certainly smalltown banks—and bankers—try to keep their relations with money-market giants like the Sloan as friendly as possible. But Mr.

221

Pomeroy could have been considering an application for a dubious loan.

"We would appreciate your cooperation, Mr. Pomeroy, in connection with this counterfeit situation we've encountered," said Thatcher.

Mr. Pomeroy's office was elderly, well-kept and conservative. So was Mr. Pomeroy. But despite appearances to the contrary, he had deep feelings. He vented them now.

"The Sloan came up here to the backwoods and ran into a pile of trouble, didn't it? Now I've headed this bank for forty-two years, and the worst I've encountered was a couple of phoney hundreds some dodos tried shipping down from Canada. We put the kibosh on that in a week. That's because we know our local people and the local territory. You just waltz in, set up shop for a couple of weeks, then go back where you came from. Stands to reason you can't protect yourself, the way we can."

Thatcher's appreciation of period pieces insulated him. But Gabler was a period piece himself.

"The reason the Sloan came in to set up shop for a couple of weeks, as you put it," he said indignantly, "is that no local bank had the facilities to handle the volume of business generated by the Olympics."

"Well, you're asking me for help," said Pomeroy waspishly, "I'm not asking you!"

Before the simmering Gabler could speed them further in the wrong direction, Thatcher intervened. "Yes, we're asking your help about that counterfeit check you spotted so promptly."

"I personally train my tellers to take a good long look at whatever they're accepting as cash," said Pomeroy disagreeably.

"The Sloan—" Everett began.

"Obviously you run a tight ship," said Thatcher, overriding him. "Now, the teller who did notice that counterfeit—"

"Wasn't a teller," Pomeroy crowed.

He enjoyed his stopper for a full minute before continuing. "*I* caught it. Always check the receipts myself. *That's* how to run a bank."

The going was difficult, and getting worse. Asking this old tartar if he had chattered was going to be an act of courage. Fortunately, Thatcher was reprieved by Pomeroy's complacency.

"As soon as I saw it, I put in a call to your manager," he said.

"Yes, we appreciated that," said Thatcher. Then, as if it were an afterthought, he began, "I don't suppose you spoke to anyone else—"

"The police!" Pomeroy snorted. "Otherwise I kept my mouth shut. Except to the tellers, that is. I went out front and took a look, because we're not in the business of cashing fakes."

"Aha, the tellers," said Everett Gabler unwisely.

In no uncertain terms, Pomeroy set him straight. The staff out front at Saranac Trust and Savings consisted of three tellers, each apparently as old and stiff-necked as Pomeroy.

"Now, what is it you're after?" he demanded.

"It was a question of who knew about that counterfeit before Bisson's murder. We thought that possibly somebody here in Saranac might have discussed it," said Thatcher with intentional vagueness.

But Pomeroy pounced. "You mean you suspected us?"

"Only of loose talk," said Thatcher before continuing. "And I don't any more." This collection of fossils was not part of the modern world.

Pomeroy was not mollified. "What about Sloan tellers?" he riposted. "I called that manager of yours. He probably shot his mouth off—" He interrupted himself to peer malevolently at Thatcher. "Never thought of that, did you?"

Thatcher could not remember what Hathaway had done after Pomeroy's first call. Had he talked to any of the tellers? And had any of the tellers talked to anybody else?

"We may have overlooked a possibility there," he said, more to himself than to his adversary.

"People who live in glass houses . . ." Pomeroy cackled.

This was more than Everett Gabler could endure. "Glass houses?" he sputtered, looking around Pomeroy's office with disdain. "Do you realize we have a staff of eighty-seven in Lake Placid alone?"

"And I suppose you're one hundred percent confident of every one of them!"

"That," Everett retorted, "is not the way large banks are run. It is not a question of knowing every single teller since birth. We will simply ascertain whether the manager did—or did not—mention this counterfeit to any of them. One telephone call will put the matter straight."

Pomeroy took him up. Thrusting a sturdy black telephone across the desk, he said, "Be my guest!"

Thatcher, who had seen this coming, was not too proud to take advantage of this gesture. "Thank you, Mr. Pomeroy, that's exactly what I'd like to do," he said, reaching across Gabler.

But more discomfiture lay in store. Roger Hathaway was not at his desk downtown. And, said the switchboard, he didn't seem to be at any of the other branches. If Mr. Thatcher wanted to leave a message, she would try . . .

"No, thank you. We'll catch him later," said Thatcher, hanging up. "And thank you, Mr. Pomeroy, for your cooperation. Everett, I think we'd better get back to Lake Placid."

"Yes indeed," said Gabler. Then, with iron self-control, he said, "It has been a pleasure to meet you, Mr. Pomeroy."

But his trials were not over. Elated by routing the city slickers, Pomeroy unbent to the extent of rising and accompanying his guests to the door.

"Still, even with all this counterfeit, I don't suppose the Sloan has exactly lost money here in the Adirondacks, has it?"

Thatcher was beginning to admire this old villain. "Well, Mr. Pomeroy, you're the man who knows how profitable the area is," he said.

To Gabler's disgust, this unscrupulous remark made a hit. Pomeroy chortled with self-satisfaction. "That I do, that I do!"

He opened the swinging door that led to the marble-floored lobby, surveyed his kingdom and dispensed largesse to those less favored than he. "Reliable help's hard to come by these days, but I like the sound of that manager—what's his name?"

"Hathaway," said Thatcher, seeing that Gabler was grinding his teeth.

"That's right, Hathaway," said Pomeroy as if Thatcher could have been mistaken. "You know, when the news carried the story about the murder, I decided I should tell him. To be honest, I didn't expect to catch him since it was after hours. But he was at the bank, working hard. That's something to take the sting off all this bad luck you've been having. There's more to running a bank than meets the eye."

He was almost kindly as he dismissed them.

On the sidewalk outside the Saranac Trust and Savings, under the big old clock, Everett let fly until Thatcher abruptly cut him short.

"Save that until later!" he said.

Gabler stared, and Thatcher nodded.

"Yes, we've been a few degrees off all morning. It's not a Saranac teller we're after, or a Sloan teller. It's a teller from Switzerland. And"—he broke off, looked up at the clock, and began to jog toward the bus stop—"we don't have any time to waste. Tilly Lowengard is going to be racing in less than an hour."

"Tilly Lowengard?" Gabler repeated, puffing after him. "What does she have to do with this?"

"We started with murder on the Olympic slopes," said Thatcher, deep in his own thoughts. "Unless we get a move on, we're going to end that way, too."

Their journey to Whiteface Mountain seemed endless. But it was just long enough for John Thatcher to outline the terrible replay he saw so clearly.

21 HIGH-PRESSURE AREA

EVEN as he explained, Thatcher was charting his immediate course of action. According to the Saranac Trust and Savings clock, according to his own wristwatch, they should reach Whiteface Mountain with a margin, dangerously small it was true, but enough to avert a second tragedy.

These calculations abruptly crashed to earth. A highway department truck on Route 86 had come to grief with a milk truck. The accident was minor, but it produced an agonizing traffic delay that ate up precious minutes. Each sweep of the second hand threw Thatcher's plans further and further out of kilter.

They were going to arrive too late to cut Tilly off at the base, too late for an orderly appeal to authority, too late for . . .

"No," said Thatcher with flat determination.

But when they pulled into the parking lot, his heart lurched. His previous visit, he realized, had been misleading. Last Saturday, with the blizzard sweeping in from the west, the peak had been wreathed in clouds, the sky had loomed low in a grey threatening pall, and the snow had begun before the slalom had been well-launched. Today a brilliant blue vault arched overhead, the air was clear and dry, visibility stretched for miles and miles. All this clarity emphasized the difficulty of the task before them.

Whiteface Mountain is not a simple, straightforward site. Towering at the northernmost end of Lake Placid Valley, it has long been a thriving ski area and, because it contains the greatest vertical drop in the eastern United States, a favorite stage for national and international events. Even in normal times the huge bulk is a complex mass of lodges, competition trails, recreational trails, lifts and support facilities. The Winter Games had added yet more ramification to the development. Signposts sprouted everywhere directing the initiate to T-bars, J-bars, chair lifts, all ascending to the intricate world four thousand feet above, with a dizzying array of place names—Cloudspin, Idiot's Delight, Calamity Lane, Easy Street.

The crackling of a loudspeaker propelled Everett Gabler into speech. "The women's slalom has begun," he said unnecessarily.

Suddenly the enemy had ceased to be a murderer crouched low in the snow, his eye glued to the crosshairs of a rifle sight. The enemy was not even the milling throng impeding movement at the base station. Now the enemy was a formidable pile of rock, throwing out shoulders and ravines, gullies and spurs, in bewildering multitude.

With immense relief, Thatcher spied a chair lift simply labeled: *Today's Slalom.*

"I'm going up to stop her," he said tightly. "Maybe I can catch her in the starting area."

Everett protested immediately. "But what about the police? We'll need them."

"And you're going to get them, I don't know how. This is where we split up, Everett."

Faced with a well-defined problem, Gabler responded automatically. Muttering something about a cruiser, he dogtrotted off to the official end of the parking lot. As he was being clamped into his seat, Thatcher blessed Everett's feel for organization. He had instinctively realized that if the police were there, a car would be there; if a car was there, a radio would be there; if a radio was there, a man would be there. What's more, he was perfectly capable of smashing a window and dealing himself into the police frequency. If anyone could possibly locate the police in this maelstrom, let alone mobilize them, Gabler was the man.

This momentary whiff of well-being was promptly snuffed out by the attendant of the double chair lift. Urging Thatcher's seatmate to make haste, he said, "C'mon, hurry up! You're going to miss half of it. The women's slalom has already begun."

The refrain was the same at the other end, while Thatcher was being unfastened.

"You folks had better step on it. Two of them have already finished. The women's slalom has begun."

But there was worse to come. Gliding through the air, Thatcher had formulated a simple program, much assisted by the recollection of Brad Withers' plans for the day. First there would be attendance at the IOC plenary session, he had said chattily over breakfast, then on to Whiteface for the final alpine event. It was witless, Thatcher recognized, for an outsider to rush around these clogged grounds looking for a contestant. But the hirelings of the IOC had experienced no difficulty plucking Gunther Euler from the middle of the ski jump and hauling him before the bar of justice. The same Draconian efficiency might save Tilly Lowengard's life. Therefore he would simply speed to Brad's side and have a couple of IOC stewards dispatched to collar her. If trumped-up charges were necessary, Thatcher never doubted his ability to produce them.

At first all went well. Brad was in full view and, as always, ready to oblige. Then came the hitch.

"But, John," Withers finally managed to break in, "this is the end of the slalom, not the beginning. This is only the Mid Station. The starting gate is up there." His hand nonchalantly encompassed empyrean heights. "The other chair lift goes all the way up. The contestants change here, depending on whether they're going to the downhill runs or the slalom runs and . . ."

His voice trailed off as he realized that his vice-president was battering his way back to the lift area. Doggedly Withers plowed after him. The trouble with John, he thought, was that he wouldn't stand still long enough for anything to be explained.

"But, John," he began, catching at a swinging arm.

"No, Brad, not now. I've got to get to the starting gate."

Withers was magnificently confident. "Well, you can't go in those clothes."

"Good God, this isn't a social occasion!"

"How are you planning to ski?"

It was enough to halt Thatcher in his tracks. "Ski?" he repeated dully.

"That's right." Withers was always willing to share his information about Olympic procedures. "I've been trying to tell you. The lift goes to the top. The starting gate is halfway down. So the competitors have to ski down to the beginning of the course."

Thatcher froze, the unwelcome news slowly sinking

in. As his gaze became openly hostile, Withers, in his turn, grew irritated. "Didn't you notice anything at all the last time you were here, John?" he demanded.

It was a home question. Thatcher cursed himself. Why hadn't he familiarized himself with the geography of Whiteface when he had the chance? He could have had a steward show him over the whole mountain. Thatcher cursed the stewards. Instead he had allowed himself to be led about blindly by young Noyes. Thatcher cursed Noyes.

In midstream, he halted. The arriving lift was just depositing another latecomer. The last object of his anathemas pushed the bar aside and clambered upright. Dick Noyes was wearing full ski gear.

He was, however, none too pleased to be spotted. "I had a good mind not to come," he announced sulkily, still smarting from his last encounter with Tilly. "If it wasn't for—"

"Shut up!" Thatcher ordered. "There's a good chance that the sniper who killed Yves Bisson is waiting for Tilly to come down the slalom run. Can you get up there and stop her?"

Dick was better with action than with words. His face was still in disarray from the shock of Thatcher's greeting, but he was already crossing over to the other chair lift.

The attendant had his own ideas. "Nobody except authorized personnel to the top," he intoned, refusing to step aside.

Brad Withers, three strides to the rear, arrived in time to confirm this policy. "This young man can't go up. I tell you what you should do, you should talk to that State Police captain, the one who—here! John!"

In one swift movement, Thatcher had transferred the

official IOC badge from Withers' chest to Noyes' wind-breaker.

"Go!" he said, allowing himself to be detained by his volubly indignant superior.

As a torrent of reproach broke over his head, he had the satisfaction of seeing Dick Noyes airborne. He felt as if he had slipped the leash of a willing but untested wolfhound. Dick, he was sure, would break every bone in his body in the effort to save Tilly. How he would fare with obstructive officialdom and confusing topography was less certain.

"I don't see what it is about that girl," complained Brad Withers, who had not stopped talking for a second. "Yesterday they were ready to blow up Whiteface so that she could race. Today everybody's going crazy trying to talk to her. First there's that policeman friend of yours, then you start acting up, now that boy is going to the top with *my* badge and what the starters are going to say about that, I don't like to think . . ."

My God, thought Thatcher, who had not finished castigating himself. Now it was going to turn out that he should always listen to what Brad had to say.

"What about that policeman friend of mine?" he asked aloud. "Do you mean that Captain Ormsby is here?"

"He's in the office at the Mid Station Lodge," Withers answered before continuing petulantly. "And that's another thing. If people want to sit around indoors, I suppose that's their business. But why come to an alpine event to do it?"

"I expect he has his reasons," said Thatcher, getting ready to shoulder his way across the Mid Station once again.

*　　*　　*

When Tilly Lowengard, head down and muscles braced, shoved her sticks into the snow and thrust herself past the electronic timer, loudspeakers blared the news of her official entry into competition.

At the Base Station Everett Gabler, posted beside a police cruiser, uncharacteristically crossed his fingers. He had succeeded in dispatching two officers, complete with skis, up to the Mid Station. But that, he had learned, was the end of the run, and Tilly's fate would have been determined before she ever reached them.

Captain Ormsby did not hear the announcement because he was inside a phone booth. When he emerged his face was drawn and he shook his head at Thatcher.

"She's already started," he reported, "and they claim she'd never even hear a recall on the PA system."

"So Noyes didn't get to her in time," Thatcher said slowly. "All we can do is hope I'm wrong about the murderer being up there."

But a scant hundred meters from the end of the course the killer was cradling a rifle, waiting for Tilly. Almost invisible in a white anorak with the hood pulled up, he was pleased she had not been the first runner. The slalom was not his event, and he had needed those trial beads to be sure, absolutely sure.

Highest of all on Whiteface, Dick Noyes had already taken the gamble of his life. He had encountered none of the problems foreseen by Thatcher at the top of the lift. His badge was an Open Sesame and, in the motley crowd of workmen generated by trail grooming and television coverage, one more anonymous man had passed without notice. It had even been easy to steal a pair of skis from the rack outside a maintenance building and set off on the slalom approach trail. The difficulty was not officialdom and not geographic confusion;

it was snow. The blizzard had left drifts of unbelievable height, and the heroic efforts to open the area had cast up further embankments. Every trail was almost a tunnel, lined by white walls of six, eight and even ten feet.

Dick, who knew far more about Olympic procedure than Thatcher, than Captain Ormsby or, for that matter, than Brad Withers, had realized all along that storming the starting building would be a protracted, self-defeating business. He had assumed that he could bypass the official corral and catch Tilly's attention as she poised for her takeoff. That was now out of the question. Bypasses today would require crampons and an ice axe.

As his skis squeaked along the churned-up approach, he considered alternatives. Days of accompanying Tilly to her practice sessions had left Dick with a built-in map of all three slalom trails. The glimmering of an idea began to emerge. The trails were widely separated at their commencement, angling together so that they converged before the Mid Station Lodge for a joint run-out area. But while one was totally independent, the two others were not. Midway along their length they kinked together and ran parallel, so closely parallel that snow could not possibly be piled between them without narrowing the trails to noncompetition standards. That area would necessarily be clear, and a skier on Mountain Run would have a clear view of Wilderness.

"Jesus Christ!"

In one heart-stopping moment the tide of realization poured over Dick Noyes. These were precisely the requirements of any hidden sniper. He, too, could not break through the ring of stewards. He, too, could not

234

go mountaineering. He, too, had to have an unobstructed view of Tilly.

And final confirmation lay just ahead where the path forked three ways. To the left there was a virgin stretch of whiteness. Dead center there was nothing but a trampled mess where competitors, timers, judges and stewards had passed on their lawful business. But on the right, as clear as writing on a blackboard, one set of skis had carved telltale tracks.

He did not hesitate for an instant. Getting to Tilly might be impossible, but getting to the killer was not. With something very close to murder in his own heart, Dick Noyes streaked rightward.

At the Lodge Thatcher cast vainly about for some form of reassurance. "They announce the halfway times," he said. "At least we'll know how she is there."

"Hell, we'll be able to see for ourselves by then," growled Ormsby. "We could see her right now, if it wasn't for all that snow."

They were standing at the top of the steps, craning their necks to see over the crowd. Flanking them were Everett's reinforcements.

"And there's not a goddam thing we can do," said one of them.

The clearing was exactly as Dick had expected. The first thing he saw was Tilly shooting around a curve with beautifully controlled precision. Then the give-away marks led his eye to an almost invisible white mound—a white mound holding a dark metal tube.

"Tilly!" Dick yelled despairingly, but it was a useless reflex and he knew it. The distance, the crackling loudspeakers, the concentration of the competitor were all against him. Neither Tilly nor the murderer had heard his voice or his rapidly nearing approach. But the figure in white had tensed slightly, shifting the rifle for some microscopic adjustment.

Without thinking Dick lofted a ski pole, twirled it javelinlike, and let fly. In the same second the pole landed, a shot rang out and Tilly awoke to her peril. All three of them responded with razor-sharp reflexes of fear, rage and frustration.

Tilly, looking neither right nor left, hunched into the tightest tuck that Dick had ever seen, increased her speed to flat-out downhill velocity and still managed to flash around the next flag without an inch to spare.

It was Dick's last sight of her. The white mound exploded into action even as his adversary glided to a halt. The rifle came up in a two-handed grip and clubbed into Dick's face before being flung aside as the murderer snatched up poles and fled down the trail.

But Dick, even with one pole and a throbbing head, was in his element. Finishing thirty-fifth in a field of thirty-six still left him ahead of almost everybody else in the world. Blinding down the course, he closed the gap in seconds and then, with every atavistic instinct at full stretch, he abandoned his remaining pole and hurled himself forward. The result was partly tackle, partly assault, and mostly simple collision. Hampered by skis and snow, the two men lay full length on the ground, clutching each other in a loverlike embrace.

And, from a distance of six inches, Dick found himself staring into the distorted features of Roger Hathaway!

At the moment every uncertainty, every resentment, every anguish of the last week boiled up in Dick Noyes for a single jubilant catharsis as his fist plowed into

Hathaway's face. Then Hathaway's hands were on his throat and he was fighting for his life.

True to Captain Ormsby's prediction, the last half of Tilly's run was visible to the spectators at the Mid Station. And they got a good deal more than they bargained for. Even her first appearance, alone, was exciting. She came flashing down the course at a do-or-die pace, flipping around the posts in a series of linked arcs that were so smooth they seemed almost absentminded.

But before the first appreciative gasps died away they were transformed into cries of surprise. Down a parallel trail, where nobody should have been, came first one skier, then a second. Hell-bent on reaching the bottom, they bashed their way forward, barely taking the turns, knocking down posts and flags, and finally colliding with each other.

"That's no way to come down a slalom run," said a disapproving voice that Thatcher recognized as Brad Withers'.

Captain Ormsby was swifter to recognize the significance of what he was seeing. "Loomis! Kantovski! Get over there!" he yelled a second before his voice would have been drowned by the cheers for Tilly's finishing time.

Dick Noyes, his eyes dimming, his ears filled with a great roaring, had been heaving and straining for a lifetime. Now, very slowly, his dazed senses were signaling a change in circumstances. He was no longer being strangled. Roger Hathaway had been pulled aside. Somebody was hanging on to him and saying the same thing, again and again.

"It's all over, kid. We've got him. You can relax now."

Gratefully Dick ceased his struggles. The heaving and the straining and the fighting for breath stopped. But the roaring did not.

"What's that noise? What's going on?"

"Didn't you hear the PA?" The trooper looked at him curiously. "Your girl friend just won the gold—and broke the world record doing it. C'mon, I'll help you up."

But Dick Noyes had fallen back on the snow, chuckling weakly, his face wreathed in a beatific smile.

22 IF WINTER COMES . . . ?

THE arrest of Roger Hathaway and the recovery of his ill-gotten gains necessarily preoccupied Thatcher and Gabler for the remainder of the afternoon. They had to sign countless documents, arrange for an interim bank manager, break the bad news to a sadly disappointed Brad Withers, and disband Milliken's operation. Nonetheless they were constantly distracted by the upheavals accompanying the final hours of the Winter Games. Mountains of sports equipment trundled by on trucks while crews maneuvered to dismantle judges' stands and electronic gear. Every conceivable facility was jammed with crowds still celebrating the U.S. hockey team's impossible dream. Commercial establishments simultaneously urged their staffs to prodigies of effort and prepared to pay them off. The kitchens of Olympic Village labored to produce a memorable farewell dinner. Suitcases began piling up in the lobbies of dormitories, motels and rented quarters. But nobody was actually leaving—not with the final gold medal awards and the formal closing ceremonies still to come that evening.

No, not even the men of the Sloan were able to tear themselves away.

"But my God, Everett, Hathaway's scheme would have been perfect if the timing had held."

The exclamation was torn from Thatcher as he stood with his party on the shores of Mirror Lake, watching the fireworks.

Everett knew exactly what he meant but regarded such remarks as antisocial. The other three were not particularly interested. In fact Gunther Euler, arriving late, had been more impressed with Tilly's accomplishments at Whiteface than anybody else's.

"What was so wonderful about Hathaway's scheme?" he now asked lazily. "One of us could have organized a gang to pass counterfeit just as well."

"You've missed the point. There never was any gang. Hathaway simply carried the counterfeit into the Sloan that evening, and effected the substitution right at the vaults." Thatcher was beginning to feel that he had been repeating these same sentences all day.

But his attempt at clarification merely bewildered the German. "If it's that easy," Euler objected, "why doesn't everybody at your bank do it?"

Everett could not resist the opportunity for a homily. "Because not everyone, young man, gives way to unbridled rapacity."

His shaft went wide of the mark. Gunther grinned down at him good-naturedly and Thatcher, reflecting on Gabler's unresting ingenuity at dreaming up new internal controls for the Sloan, intervened.

"That, of course, is one reason," he agreed diplomatically. "The other is, for a barefaced theft like that, detection is almost as simple as execution. Probably the temptation does idly cross the minds of some of our employees. Then they realize that they're bound to be caught and dismiss the idea. Unfortunately Roger Hathaway chose another route. He set to work devising ways to obscure the issue. That's why he needed Yves Bisson."

At last he had captured the attention of his other two companions. Tilly, who had been moving in a quiet cloud of fulfillment ever since standing to attention for the Swiss national anthem, said, "What an unlikely combination! It never occurred to me that they knew each other."

Dick, who had been resting from the emotional buffets of the day by clasping Tilly's hand and thinking of absolutely nothing, returned to reality.

"You could have knocked me down with a feather when I realized the guy I was tangling with was Roger," he admitted.

Rarely had a figure of speech been less appropriate. Dick Noyes had been knocked down all right, but a bulldozer was closer to the operative agent. And Roger Hathaway now looked even worse. After the police had pried them apart, the first stop had been the Medical Center, followed in Hathaway's case by an emergency visit to the dentist.

"They went at each other like a pair of wildcats," Ormsby had reported to Thatcher. "My boys tell me they never saw anything like it. Those two could barely move, being down in the snow with their skis still on, but that didn't stop them from trying to kill each other."

It was not surprising that the damage had been to extremities. Hathaway was missing two front teeth, while Dick Noyes' black eye covered one side of his face and his right hand was stiff with bandages. But for Dick, at least, the catharsis had been effective. He sounded almost detached as he began to pelt Thatcher with questions.

"Why did he need somebody like Yves? Roger was the one who knew about banking."

"True enough. But Hathaway's whole objective was to make the crime look as if it had been committed by someone outside the banking system, and long before any Eurochecks reached the Sloan tellers. He was performing a conjuring act, the most important element of which was misdirection. You must remember he chose a European instrument to forge and an international event at which to pass the counterfeit. To add further substance to the illusion, he wanted some innocent foreigners caught in the act of cashing fakes. In short, Hathaway intended to bathe the entire theft in such an overseas atmosphere that the authorities would start on the wrong foot immediately."

"If you say so." Dick's furrowed brow made this statement more a grudging concession than wholehearted agreement. "Then Yves' only part in the whole deal was to run around the Village switching a couple of checks whenever he got the chance?"

Thatcher shook his head. "His role was much more central than that. Bisson was ideally situated at his travel agency not only to swindle a few tour groups, but to choose charters that began their trip at Lake Placid before going on to other cities. And I doubt if his activities in the Village were as casual as you think. I'm sure he made an effort to select athletes who were planning further travel. We've already heard about one who was going on to the West Coast and another who was continuing to Japan. Hathaway wanted to reinforce his plan with geographic dispersal of the fakes."

"The way you describe it, it sounds surefire. But you

caught on to Roger, didn't you?" Dick blurted, coming to the root of his objection. "So it wasn't such a wonderful scheme after all."

"I neglected to mention the other essential ingredient in Hathaway's script. It was all this," said Thatcher, waving an arm broadly.

His gesture encompassed the scene before them—the thousands of spectators lining the lakeside, the flags flying in massed array, the torches whose flickering beams were reflected by the ice, the band playing its penultimate selection.

"Under Hathaway's original timetable, he was like a man committing a crime in a city that's due to be hit by a nuclear bomb. Clues, witnesses and victims will all be blown sky high. This little world that has been created in Lake Placid is very temporary. Do you realize that, if Hathaway's substitution had taken place today, the Telex operators at the Sloan would only now be realizing that something was wrong? By the time the police began asking questions, this little world would have disappeared, scattered to the four corners of the globe. And for weeks fake Eurochecks would be surfacing in Washington and New York and Los Angeles. Small wonder if the authorities believed a major European ring was operating in the United States."

"And all this fell flat because Yves made a mechanical mistake in paying for a snowmobile?"

Gunther Euler sounded so regretful that he would inevitably have drawn Everett Gabler's fire if the field had not already been preempted.

"Hathaway is a fool," Everett said severely. "To develop such a plan and fail to abide by it!"

"He is certainly an incorrigible optimist," Thatcher began before the blank faces of his audience told him they were not following. He realized he would have to explain in more detail. "Timing was too critical a factor in the plot to be dispensed with. After Hathaway received that warning from the bank at Saranac, he should have told Bisson to play the injured innocent and abandoned the whole attempt."

Tilly shook her head sadly. "Instead of which he decided he couldn't rely on Yves and therefore had to kill him."

Thatcher thought of Roger Hathaway's talking jag at the police station—the words tumbling out in a torrent of grievance, justification, self-exoneration. Nobody was supposed to be hurt, he had said over and over again. Murder had never entered his mind. But what else could he do? Everything had gone wrong, the fates had conspired against him, and it just wasn't fair.

"That's what Hathaway says and, for all I know, he believes it. But I don't. I think he was consumed by the goal of that half-million beyond common sense, beyond prudence and beyond humanity. No matter what the cost, he was unwilling to stop. And on the surface, the murder seemed to accomplish its purpose. If anything, the disclosures about Yves Bisson tended to support the European theory. Nonetheless Everett is right. It was a colossal mistake. It gave the police, and the Sloan, a breathing space while witnesses were still available. Captain Ormsby was able to isolate the Saranac incident, we were able to bring in Milliken's crew, and the perpetrator was identified as a member of the Olympic family. On top of all that the blizzard arrived, freezing everybody into place for an additional forty-eight hours."

Tilly had been listening intently to every word, a puzzled frown growing by the minute. "Let me see if I've got this straight," she said quietly. "You thought the criminal was a European, that it was someone who went snowmobiling at Saranac, and somebody who knew more about banking procedures than Yves Bisson. Mr. Thatcher, did you suspect me of being a murderer?"

There was nothing for it but to tell the truth. "I did wonder," he confessed ruefully. "Particularly after your first performance at Whiteface. I thought perhaps you had drugged yourself in order to have an excuse for fleeing."

The storm broke over his head immediately. Dick Noyes and, surprisingly, Gunther were both outraged.

"You've got to be crazy! Tilly shoot somebody in cold blood?" Dick gasped. "You only have to look at her."

Everett's meticulously organized exculpation was brutally brushed aside.

"You're like all the rest," Gunther charged. "It's easier to find a scapegoat than to clean up the mess."

"Do you realize she could have killed herself on Whiteface? That course isn't for babies."

The only calm one was Tilly, and it took her some time to restrain her supporters. "Well, at least it's a logical explanation for my being drugged," she was able to say at last. "And it's the first one I've heard. I still don't know why it happened."

Thatcher's notion that Tilly was quicker-witted than her companions was confirmed. Everett, of course, did not have to fall back on native endowment. He firmly believed that anybody employed by a bank could achieve a level of rational analysis denied his fellows. Roger Hathaway was simply the exception that proved the rule.

"Hathaway was in a panic," Thatcher explained. "You see, he made his substitution in the vault as quickly as possible, which meant that most of the counterfeits had already been signed with fictitious names. Milliken and his crew could have looked forever for Ludwig Mueller and Etienne Dumont and Elsa Grunbacher. But it would have been overly suspicious if none of the payees was identifiable. So Hathaway brought along a handful of blanks that night and filled in the names of athletes at Olympic Village who had cashed bona fide checks that day. Of course under his original plan the athletes would have been long gone before questions were asked. But under the new circumstances he came a cropper in at least two cases. With a West German, he signed the wrong denomination. But you were the real problem."

"Why?" Tilly demanded, exasperated. "It wasn't as if I was the only one complaining that my check was good. He told me himself everybody was saying the same thing."

Thatcher smiled at her. "He was lying. Everybody else was making a general statement they couldn't support. You were very specific. In the first place, you could follow your check from issuance to the moment of cashing and kept records to prove it had the same number all the way. Second, unlike most of the others, you cashed it at the Sloan instead of a commercial establishment. So there was no grey area for hanky-panky. And finally, your worst offense, I am afraid, was that you work for a bank. Given enough time to concentrate, you were bound to figure out the substitution had occurred on the other side of the teller's counter. Really, all things considered, it's surprising that Hathaway didn't try to throttle you on the spot."

The pleasantry misfired. It would be a long time before Tilly Lowengard recognized any material for badinage in her encounter with Roger Hathaway.

"Oh yes?" she said, tossing her head so violently that Dick removed his injuries to a safe distance. "I'd have liked to see him try. But shooting from ambush and poison were more his style."

Everett was every bit as serious. "The data supports your view. And of course he had to work with what was at hand. He happened to have his allergy medicine so he dosed you with an indiscriminate amount and hoped for the best. I suppose, John, that is what you meant by calling him an incorrigible optimist."

"Yes. Every threat to Hathaway produced a spur-of-the-moment response that ignored wider implications. He killed Bisson on that principle instead of back pedaling. With Tilly, he didn't care if she crashed on the slope or was expelled from the Olympics—so long as she went away. Naturally he didn't bargain on the storm making her removal impossible."

"He didn't bargain on Bernard or Egon either," Dick said, beginning to cheer up.

"Who could?" Thatcher retorted, but even as the words left his mouth he was having second thoughts. With individual affirmative action on the rise, the range of probabilities in any given situation had expanded alarmingly.

The young men burst into loud guffaws at the recollection of Melville dangling helplessly over Whiteface. Tilly recalled them to order once more. To her the aftermath of her expulsion was not high jinks with cable cars, but a baffling period of safety exploding into sudden peril.

"I still don't understand why Roger Hathaway tried to shoot me at the end. After all, I'd been here for over two days after he drugged me. We met each other at the disco a couple of times, nothing happened, and then, out of the blue, he wants to kill me."

Thatcher set himself to correcting this egocentric approach. "Quite a lot happened, although it did not appear to involve you. From Hathaway's viewpoint the drugging had worked. You had other things to think about, and your supporters assumed a competitor was responsible. Nonetheless he was slowly going mad as he watched the progress of the investigation."

The athletes were all members of their own generation, adhering to its shibboleths and conventions as rigorously as any young Victorian. To them it was axiomatic that officialdom, most especially the police, was inept at best and corrupt at worst.

"What progress?" scoffed Euler. "The police kept harping on that trip to Twin Forks and Hathaway wasn't even there!"

Gabler frowned at him. "Considering that of the seven survivors from that trip, five were busily suppressing certain facets of their activities, it is scarcely surprising the police were misled."

"You're underestimating Captain Ormsby's results," Thatcher added more temperately. "By concentrating on the Saranac trip he managed to extract a damagingly clear account of Yves Bisson's last day, quite apart from reducing the number of suspects. But what was really tearing Hathaway apart was the Sloan's performance. We had managed to get a crew into Lake Placid just before the blizzard, and they spent forty-eight hours cross-examining all the athletes and sales clerks who would have been unavailable under the original timetable."

Dick Noyes had an objection. "Roger didn't look like he was coming apart at the seams to me."

"In his position it was normal to be very worried. He was a bank manager sitting on top of a major loss. But consider what he had to put up with. He had to stand there and watch while the European theory went down the drain, while Everett and I gradually became convinced that the murderer was part of the Olympic family, while Milliken proved that substitutions occurred after Eurochecks were cashed in stores. By the time you delivered the death blows in the bank this morning, he was already desperate."

Dick and Tilly were dumfounded. For them the scene in the bank was already a towering personal landmark—their first quarrel, and one of such shattering dimensions it had threatened their entire future.

"What did it have to do with Roger?" Dick asked as resentfully as if Hathaway had intruded into the bedroom.

"I barely noticed he was there," said Tilly with patent sincerity.

Slowly Thatcher listed the damning items they had been too preoccupied to notice. "Hathaway knew that German marks and French francs were going to be investigated before Swiss francs. He thought he had some time in hand until Tilly marched up to the counter and told the world that her first Eurocheck had been good right up to the moment it reached a Sloan teller. On top of that, she had acquired far too much information about the chemical analysis of her specimen. Enough to exonerate her competition and narrow down the group that could possibly have drugged her."

Tilly was staring at him. "But I narrowed it down to the ones who were at Saranac."

"Yes, and promptly appealed to Hathaway for confirmation because he was sitting right beside you," Thatcher reminded her. "Whereupon Dick drew the proper conclusion that the murderer had drugged you. No wonder Hathaway urged you to go ahead and race. He had decided to kill you before Milliken got to you

—particularly when it came out that you weren't even leaving the country, but going to Colorado instead."

"Yes, she is," Dick said proudly. "We're flying out tomorrow."

This was quite enough to divert both of them.

"Dick says I'll love it." Tilly was so excited she was unconsciously yanking and twisting the gold medal still draped around her neck. "It seems it's just like Switzerland."

From their dossiers Thatcher knew that Dick had never been in Europe and Tilly had never been west of New York. How had they ever managed to come up with this conclusion?

"There are mountains and snow," Tilly continued rhapsodically, "and pastures filled with Holsteins."

Suddenly Richard Noyes, Doctor of Veterinary Medicine, emerged.

"No," he said firmly. "Not dairy cattle. Beef cattle."

For a moment Tilly faltered. But then, "Well, I expect it's all the same," she concluded buoyantly.

Thatcher decided he had been too captious. To the eyes of young love, Colorado and Switzerland probably were identical. Gunther Euler's eyes, however, had been fixed unwaveringly on Roger Hathaway's get-rich-quick scheme. He was the only one not satisfied by Thatcher's recitation.

"I understand what Hathaway did," he said heavily. "But how did you find out? You must have known when you went to Whiteface to warn Tilly."

"Oh, yes," Thatcher agreed. "I'm only surprised that we didn't tumble to it sooner. There was never any doubt about the qualifications of the murderer. He had to be able to ski, he had to have some knowledge of the financial system, he had to have sufficient European connections to contact Bisson and, of course, he had to be a man who wanted money."

He came under fire from three directions at once.

"No wonder you didn't think of Roger," said Dick. Then, before this could be mistaken as a tribute to character, he scraped his chin reflectively and went on. "The guy I was chasing was such a good skier I never figured it could be anyone that old."

"Why should he need money?" queried Tilly. "I thought he had a promising future at the Sloan. Wasn't the Lake Placid job a plum?"

"How could he have European connections? He gave up skiing before he was international class," Gunther objected.

Thatcher stared them all down. "The man who ambushed Yves Bisson had to be at home on skis, he did not have to be a champion. And there are other forms of foreign experience besides competitive athletics. Hathaway had been stationed at the Sloan's London branch for several years. During that period he went to winter sports resorts on the continent. We all know he was at Innsbruck. He had ample opportunity to meet Bisson."

Gunther and Dick were silenced, but not Tilly. "You said he needed money," she persisted.

"I said he wanted money." Thatcher paused, then saw an obvious parallel. "In the course of investigating Yves Bisson we heard a good deal about young athletes being exposed to the jet set and wanting to become a permanent part of it. The same could be said of Roger Hathaway. While he was in London he was married to a rich wife, moved in a circle of rich people, took part in the golden life. All that came to an end with his divorce, and he was back to working for a living. Yes, you were right when you said he had a promising future, but he wasn't willing to wait for it. He wanted a golden present."

The opportunity for moralizing was irresistible to Everett Gabler. "An unhealthy attitude for a young banker, as well as a young athlete," he remarked to the surrounding countryside. "Look where it has led Hathaway."

Given the provocation, Gunther Euler was mildness itself. "At least this athlete doesn't think in terms of robbery and murder. I leave that to you bankers. And as long as I don't break any laws and I don't hurt anybody, I don't see why you should complain if I make a good thing out of my ski jumping."

His untroubled assurance was a far cry from the defiant cockiness he had exhibited that morning, and Tilly was swift to guess the reason. "Gunther! Does that mean your deal with Wennerdonk's is going through?"

"They showed the ninety-meter live on German television, and that made me a national hero." Euler grinned broadly. "Herr Wennerdonk and I signed the contract at dinner just now."

Tilly was delighted. "But how wonderful! Why in the world didn't you tell us?"

"Because you were getting a gold medal, Tilly. I wasn't going to butt in on your big moment."

Not for the first time Thatcher noticed that success sweetens almost everybody's disposition. But Gunther Euler was still a novice at consideration for others and, when Tilly vented her feelings by hugging him violently, he was relieved to return to the business at hand.

"All right," he said sternly enough to cover his recent lapse, "you've said that Hathaway could meet the qualifications. But how did you pinpoint him? Especially with the police concentrating on Saranac?"

"That concentration paid off. Captain Ormsby was working on the assumption there was no reasonable way for the murderer to learn of Bisson's mistake except through seeing it. But when Coach Vaux was questioned after his arrest, he produced a surprising observation. He said that Yves Bisson had stopped worrying the night before his murder. Ormsby was willing to modify his original opinion. He reasoned that perhaps Bisson had confided in his confederate and been reassured."

Dick Noyes jumped in too quickly. "Then that let us off the hook."

"It did a good deal more," Thatcher told him. "It left me speculating what that reassurance could have been. But the penny didn't drop until we went to Saranac. We were wondering if a bank employee there could have been the conduit of information to the killer."

Tilly's eyes were sparkling with appreciation. "I bet I know what that reassurance was," she announced. "Yves and Roger both thought the fake check would come into the Sloan."

"Precisely." Thatcher beamed at her ready comprehension. "Almost all foreign currency in the Lake Placid area was ending up at the Sloan branches. Hathaway wasn't seriously worried by Bisson's mistake. He intended to stop that check before it caused trouble. Then, when he got the call from Saranac, he panicked, deciding to kill Bisson and go through with his substitution that very night."

By the time that Gunther puzzled his way through this explanation, he was feeling disgruntled. "And that was enough? To cross everybody else off and settle on Hathaway?"

"Almost everybody else was already crossed off. You

and the Antonellis had had other fish to fry. Vaux and Miss Maas were explained. Tilly was doing her level best to stay in the Olympics." Thatcher ticked off the names one by one. "I don't say it was enough to arrest the man. But when we learned that he was already doing night work at the Sloan when Pomeroy called him the second time, when we remembered that his quarters at the Andiron Inn were isolated enough to allow him to run in for skis without being observed, then the fact that he had gone missing—just when Tilly was about to race—rang a loud clear warning. All we could do was pray that we'd get to Whiteface in time."

"But you did. And then you got Dick," Tilly chanted happily, "and Dick got Roger."

"What's more, I take back what I said about your skiing, Dick," said Gunther Euler in handsome apology. "You didn't look bad chasing Hathaway."

"Isn't everything grand!"

Thatcher hoped that Tilly was not going to press her desire for happy endings any further. He could reassure her about Coach Vaux. That wily opportunist was getting off with a suspended sentence, and Katarina Maas would ride on his coattails. But what rosy sunset could be produced for Roger Hathaway?

Fortunately new arrivals claimed their attention. "Tilly, we've been looking all over for you. We want to congratulate you."

"Thank you, Bernard." Tilly was a girl who remembered her manners. "And Egon, you got a bronze in the fifty-kilometer. Isn't our team doing well today!"

Bernard Heise looked at her piercingly. "They say you're not going back with us, you're going to stay with Dick's family. Does that mean I should congratulate him, too?"

Tilly blushed. "We're not sure yet. Dick still has a

year of school, but we don't want to wait." She turned to Thatcher. "I've been meaning to ask you, Mr. Thatcher. Do you think there's a bank in Colorado where I could get a job?"

Thatcher, mentally reviewing a list of the Sloan's correspondents, said that it seemed to him quite possible. But before Tilly could demand the list, as he was convinced she would, there was a brave flourish from the band. The last medals had been awarded, the last speeches were over, the last song had been sung. And now it was time for the final act of the Winter Games of 1980. In deference to the departing Olympic flame, the electric lights went out and then, one by one, the encircling torches were extinguished. The lake and its tiny community returned to the mountains in which they were cradled.

The ensuing hush did not last long enough.

From the velvety darkness issued a youthful pronouncement. "You must not work for a bank, Tilly. Let Hathaway be a lesson to you. Financial institutions like these contaminate everyone they touch. Something will have to be done about it."

Everett Gabler sucked in his breath with a hiss as he visualized Bernard and Egon let loose on the Sloan. Thatcher decided to take more positive steps.

"You don't know the half of it, Heise," he said gravely. "You will find, when you continue your researches in Zurich, that the international gold and monetary markets need reformation as well."

Switzerland had raised this young man. Let Switzerland cope with him.